*Para: Gabo,*
*Gracias por tu [...]*
*Espero lo dist[...]*

# ANOTHER WORLD

*Amor, Sabiduría y Voluntad*

Written and Illustrated by:

# UNLOCK THE SECRETS OF ANOTHER WORLD: OWN THE ART, EMBRACE THE MAGIC

Dive into the enchanting universe of *Another World* with our exclusive NFT collection. Each piece in this collection features the original artwork that brought the captivating story of *Another World* to life. By owning these unique NFTs, you're not just collecting art—you're becoming part of a new movement, helping to spread the knowledge that the extraordinary realms of *Another World* are more than just fantasy. Embrace the magic, join the community, and let the world know that Another World is a reality waiting to be discovered.

*https://opensea.io/collection/another-world-the-book*

Dreams only come true...
...upon awakening

# DEDICATION

This book is really a collection of remarkable events from our planet Earth, many of which remain unknown to most. To all the pioneers whose work is highlighted within these pages—your contributions have been a beacon of inspiration and a guiding reference. If any of the facts in this book spark your curiosity, or seem too extraordinary to be true, I encourage you to explore the lives of these remarkable individuals. You might find that reality is even more fascinating than fiction.

In alphabetical order:

Adamski, George
Atkinson, William Walker,
Blavatzky, Helena
Bruno, Giordano
Cayce, Edgar
Campbell, Thomas
Emoto, Masaru
Fleischmann, Martin
Sagan, Carl
Schauberger, Viktor
Pons, Stanley
Rosenberg, Marshall
Rousseau, Jean-Jacques
Luque Álvarez, Josefa Rosalía

# GLOSSARY OF HUNUMAN TERMS IN ALPHABETICAL ORDER

**Ákuah:** Water

**Boehara:** Chair Professor

**Bham-yi:** Energy-based creatures that represent the habits, customs, and even vices of people. Usually with a viscous and sticky appearance, their shapes and sizes are varied, generally related to the energy they seem to feed on through energetic threads attached to their host.

**Conjunctions:** Time range equivalent to 5 Fifths in which the Hunuman Cycle is divided

**Cycles:** The time it takes Hunum to complete an orbit around Thías. Equivalent in number to Earth years because of the similarities in size and location of both planets with respect to their respective suns.

**Dahna:** Refered to Dahna, Hunum´s moon. Night

**Dahnivages:** They wander during the dahna (see above)

**Debos:** Akuahgrandian currency

**Dimenium:** Hunuman name for Deuterium, an isotope of hydrogen

**Drapo:** Hunuman animal popularly used by hunumans as pets.

**Eco Synthesis:** Physical chemical process similar to cold fusion

**Ecuaniums:** Neutrons

**Essential Particles:** Hunuman name for molecules

**Gaemo:** One of the names given to God in Hunum.

**Galar / Galera:** Galar (male) Galera (female): A term of respect used to address a person who is senior in age, dignity, or position.

**Ghori:** Hunuman number

**Globanet:** Information and Communications Network, analogous to the terrestrial Internet

**Haloguín:** Symphonic hunuman musical instrument, composed of strings that range from a metal spiral to a hollow wooden base. It is played with bows in both hands simultaneously.

**Halure:** Helium

**Hyla:** Analogous to LASER

**Informatist:** Hunuman profession that involves the acquisition, processing, interpretation, and dissemination of information through any written, oral, visual, or graphic medium.

**Krono:** Device to measure time.

**Kulka:** Instrument of torture and execution used in ancient times in Hunum (similar to the Earthly gallows). For the religion that dominated in that region of the planet, the Kulka was, paradoxically, adored and venerated as a holy symbol, because it was where the Messiah was executed, giving her life for hunumanity.

**Magnhuno:** Leader of a nation elected by popular vote.

**Mega Rays:** X Rays

**Munai:** Title for those who achieved the highest academic degree.

**Nanomic:** Referred to hunuman particles called nanoms, atoms.

**Nanonets:** Electrons

**Nanosols:** Protons

Nokó: Electronic communication device.

**Nomocat:** Diplomatic title in Akhuagrandia and other countries in Hunum who represent the interests of the people and is responsible for making, debating, and voting on laws, and also overseeing the actions of the other members of the government.

**Ohmas Number:** Hunumans also possess knowledge of what we, Earthlings, know as the golden number, 1.618033, which in turn gives rise to the golden ratio and golden spiral—all of which are present as numerical and geometric patterns in nature and are used as symbols of beauty in the arts.

**Openness:** Equivalent to the Liberal or Left-Wing faction on Earth

**Perie:** Hunuman number

**Proccuan:** Hunuman equivalent of a portable personal computer

**Qelca:** Multi-purpose electronic device that is designed to meet individual needs regarding information handling.

**Quint:** A unit of time composed of five thías

**RB:** Remote Broadcast, analogous to TV technology. The receiving device is called BR (Broadcast Receiver)

**Thermos:** Temperature Measurement unit

**Thías:** Refers to the Hunuman sun. Day.

**Thíaset:** The color orange

**Trisfacio:** Hunuman name for Hydrogen

**Ucceno:** Oxygen

# GLOSSARY OF HUNUMAN TERMS IN ORDER OF APPEARANCE

**Cycles:** The time it takes Hunum to complete an orbit around Thías. Equivalent in number to Earth years, due to the similarities in size and location of both planets with respect to their respective suns.

**Thías:** Referred to the hunuman sun. Day

**Dahna:** Referred to Dhana, Hunum's moon. Night

**Haloguín:** Symphonic hunuman musical instrument, composed of strings that range from a metal spiral to a hollow wooden base. It is played with bows in both hands simultaneously.

**Dahnivages:** They wander during the dahna (see above)

**Ákuah:** Water

**Globanet:** Information and Communications Network, analogous to the terrestrial Internet

**RB:** Remote Broadcast, analogous to TV technology. The receiving device is called BR (Broadcast Receiver)

**Quint:** A unit of time composed of five thías

**Nokó:** Electronic communication device.

**Krono:** Device to measure time

**Gaemo:** One of the names given to God in Hunum.

**Galar / Galera:** Galar (male) Galera (female): A term of respect used to address a person who is senior in age, dignity, or position.

**Bham-yi:** Energy-based creatures that represent the habits, customs, and even vices of people. Usually with a viscous and sticky appearance, their shapes and sizes are varied, generally related to the energy they seem to feed on through energetic threads attached to their host.

**Munai:** Title for those who achieved the highest academic degree.

**Magnhuno:** Leader of a nation, commonly elected by vote.

**Informatist:** Hunuman profession that involves the acquisition, processing, interpretation, and dissemination of information through any written, oral, visual, or graphic medium.

**Ghori:** Hunuman number

**Debos:** Akuahgrandian currency

**Eco Synthesis:** Physical chemical process similar to cold fusion

**Boehara:** Chair Professor

**Kulka:** Cruel instrument of torture and execution used in ancient times in Hunum (similar to the Earthly gallows). For the religion that dominated in that region of the planet, the Kulka was, paradoxically, adored and venerated as a holy symbol, because it was where their Messiah was executed, giving their life for them.

**Drapo:** Hunuman animal popularly used by hunumans as pets

**Nomocat:** Diplomatic title in Akhuagrandia and other countries in Hunum who represent the interests of the people and is responsible for making, debating, and voting on laws, and also overseeing the actions of the other members of the government.

**Conjunctions:** Time range equivalent to 5 Fifths in which the Hunuman Cycle was divided

**Thíaset:** Color orange

**Qelca:** Multi-purpose electronic device that is designed to meet individual needs regarding information handling.

**Perie:** Hunuman number

**Openness:** Equivalent to the Liberal or Left-Wing faction on Eart

**Proccuan:** Hunuman equivalent to a portable personal computer

**Dimenium:** Hunuman name for Deuterio

**Essential Particles:** Hunuman name for molecules.

**Trisfacio**: Hunuman name for Hydrogen.

**Nanomic:** Referred to nanoms, atoms

**Nanosols:** Protons

**Nanonets:** Electrons

**Hyla:** Analog to LASER

**Ucceno:** Hunuman name for Oxygen

**Ecuaniums:** Neutron

**Thermos:** Temperature Measurement unit

**Mega Rays:** X Rays

**Halure:** Helium

**Ohmas Number:** Hunumans also possess knowledge of what we, Earthlings, know as the golden number, 1.618033, which in turn gives rise to the golden ratio and golden spiral—all of which are present as numerical and geometric patterns in nature and are used as symbols of beauty in the arts.

# TABLE OF CONTENTS

Preface ................................................................................................ 1

Chapter I.        The Sense in Nonsense ..................................................... 3

Chapter II.       Searching for Answers is an Inside Job ............................ 29

Chapter III.      Unveiling ...................................................................... 57

Chapter IV.       A Dream to Awaken ..................................................... 71

Chapter V.        Before Birth ................................................................. 87

Chapter VI.       Following the Thread ................................................... 95

Chapter VII.      The Secret Is In The Ákuah ......................................... 135

Chapter VIII.     Together Again, Well, almost… .................................. 155

Chapter IX.       Visible War, Invisible War ........................................... 167

Chapter X.        An Unexpected End .................................................... 181

Epilogue ......................................................................................... 187

# PREFACE

*https://opensea.io/collection/another-world-the-book*

Many, many billion light-years from the disk of the Milky Way, far beyond the last star visible through Earth's most powerful telescopes, lies Pronos, a galaxy that shares striking similarities to our own. Cradle of thousands of suns, Thías is the smallest of all. A tiny yellow star, guardian of seven planets: Morú, Volux, Hunum, Zax, Jurus, Kalwais, and Leyán. Of all these, only the third, Hunum, had the necessary conditions to support life as we know it. Life that thrived, perfectly suited to the diverse landscapes of the planet. Mighty rivers with their akuahfalls cascade from great heights, creating endless rainbows that wrap around the surrounding nature. Dense jungles, brimming with exotic wildlife and vegetation, immerse observers in a realm of deep green shades and enigmatic sounds. Deserts stretch wide and unforgiving, with their dunes shaped by the wind, revealing a subtle beauty in the harshness under the blazing sun. Mountains with icy peaks soar towards the sky, offering sanctuary to remarkable creatures adapted to survive the eternal dusk of high altitudes. Archipelagos sketch the outlines of oceans with beaches of multicolored sands and crystal-clear akuahs, standing as serene havens in a world that never rests. However, all of these marvels seem of little importance to its inhabitants, the hunas and hunos. Looking very similar to Earth's women and men, they suffered from the same myopia before the beauty of their ship-home, and like them, lived as many other beings from many other planets in the universe… They lived unaware. Consequently, Hunum was a planet divided by the same shadows that darken Earth – Bordered nations, monetary system and exploitation, armies in constant tension, divergent religions and beliefs, and the relentless pursuit of possessions and power over others; in short, divisions and suffering… Thus, an extremely sick planet on the verge of self-destruction. As you might imagine then, the stories unfolding on Hunum were very similar to those on our Earth and perhaps for this reason, you may find echoes of terrestrial realities within the narratives contained in these pages… yet, it will be purely the work of – coincidence – (if by the end of our tale you are still convinced that such a thing truly exists).

# CHAPTER I

## THE SENSE IN NONSENSE

Mae-uhkel had been hiding his condition for many cycles... perhaps too many. A slender huno, with his dark skin, typical of the native race from those latitudes of the planet, lived in a humble home in a popular neighborhood in the capital of a small country in the north of Hunum, called Akuahgrandia. His abundant curly black hair, as black as his eyes, fell over his prominent cheekbones, framing his soft, rounded jaw, giving him the appearance of an ordinary young hunuman. But nothing could be further from the truth. Behind his simple and ordinary appearance, Mae-uhkel hid a strange secret from the world. It started in his early childhood when imaginary friends shared endless hours of games and adventures under the tender but skeptical gaze of his mother, who overlooked all of this as nothing more than the product of a vivid imagination. Little Mae-uhkel soon adopted this dismissive attitude from his mother as his own, thus beginning his conflict. As he grew up, these seemingly innocent experiences, easy to disregard at first, began to change; they became more confusing, more frequent, more impactful, and significant, which started to worry Mae-uhkel, who was now entering his adolescence. His anxiety and restlessness were due not only to the gradual transformation in the tone of his experiences but also to his growing awareness of the outcome they might be predicting for him, a dark fate outlined by a ghost from the past that haunted him relentlessly. The tragic story of his father, a simple worker from Akuahgrandia with a peculiar condition that led him to spend his last thías confined in a mental institution, diagnosed with schizophrenia. The grave sentence that this medical verdict meant for the poor huno plunged him into a cycle of depression and self-imposed isolation. He increasingly refused to be visited in the detention center, deepening his suffering, and worsening his state. This whole picture ended tragically on the dahna he decided to take his own life when Mae-uhkel was still just a boy. Now he understood better the reason behind his mother's attitude. It was a desperate attempt to convince herself and him that it was all the product of his imagination and not psychotic hallucinations.

The shadow of this doom thus loomed large over the young huno as he grew up. The fear that his delirious spasms were factually early symptoms of a hereditary and potentially very destructive insanity turned him into a reserved, taciturn, and insecure huno who found solace only in his readings, his studies, and the music of his haloguín[1].

That dahna was clear and calm. Only the sounds of the dahnivages[2] animals intermittently interrupted the peaceful silence. Then, once again, it happened to him. A multicolored mist slowly surrounded him, becoming denser and lifting him lightly off the ground in synchrony with sweet chords produced by strange harmonic sounds that further beautified the environment. From floating statically to feeling in slow motion at first, he gradually gained speed. Emerging from the colorful fog, he saw himself alongside multiple ships of various shapes: spherical, lenticular, cylindrical, conical... all moving in an aerial choreography across a violet sky colored with magenta clouds. At the same time, on the surface, some beings who looked like people, with stylized faces and bodies were spread everywhere, laughing, and chatting cheerfully. Although strange with their polychromatic hair and skins, he felt them familiar in some way. In the distance, a majestic, amber-colored building stood out among the violet mist. With a strange symbol on its crest, the bucolic structure rose like a giant sentinel on the top of a steep hill, and from its heart sprang a spring of ákuah[3] that became an akuahfall, showering its mist over the peaceful valley filled with lush and exuberant nature, finally ending in a crystalline stream that was the drinking hole for strange animals and also the unnoticed route

---

1    Symphonic hunuman musical instrument, composed of strings that range from a metal spiral to a hollow wooden base. It is played with bows in both hands simultaneously.

2    They wander during the dahna (night)

3    Water

for his flight. Now at the foot of the imposing akuahfall, he soared over and upstream it in a low flight, reaching the outskirts of what seemed to be a ceremonial temple.

*https://opensea.io/collection/another-world-the-book*

Despite the beautiful rainbow framing the entrance, suggesting a splendid welcoming portal, it was the symbol crowning the sanctuary that caught his attention. He stared at it while continuing his glide; the memory of a recurring appearance fluttered in his mind, and while he wandered through his memories reviewing all the other occasions the insignia had crossed his path during his life, he heard a sweet voice that pulled him from his thoughts:

"Ghel-dar!, my ghel-dar!" Just as one of the ships flew beside him too close... triggering a warning sound?!... it was the annoying alarm, indicating it was time to get up. Yesterday he had arrived late to work, and his supervisor had not liked it at all. He had overslept for the first time in the cycle... well, second... but it was not an unforgivable fault... It was just so hard for him to get out of bed, where he enjoyed those last moments wrapped in the fluffy sheets... Still unable to open his eyes, his heavy body tried to awaken, but his mind continued to go over the dream from which he had just returned.

"The same dream, the same symbol, but... what is 'mightbheldar'? It is the first time I've heard that word, something more to investigate" he thought, still drowsy; after a deep yawn, he continued:

"All I want now is to keep sleeping, dreaming that I'm gliding" he said with a sigh, turning over in bed for a few moments; he would have preferred to remain in the warmth of his sheets, enveloped in the harmony and beauty of that dream rather than face another thía of coldness, harshness, and chaos in the 'real' world... but he thought... "I better wake up once and for all, or my supervisor will surely make me fly, but with a kick out the door, 'Late again, Granahoi!?... There is nothing left to clean here, if you want, you can go back home and work via GlobaNet...'" he said, imitating his supervisor, the director of the maintenance department of the RB[4] Station where Mae-uhkel worked. After his customary contortionist stretch, the tall young huno ran his hands through his abundant curly hair, rumpled himself, and jumped out of bed. His room was his personal refuge; next to his bedroom door, a mat lay on the floor. He practiced Bayheme, a discipline consisting of assuming different body poses with synchronized breathing. His mother insistently taught him to do this from an early age. She used to say it favored his lucidity by stimulating his concentration as well as provided much needed physical activity and flexibility. But this small rug was not the most unusual thing in the room of a boy his age. What really made it stand out was one very particular wall, the largest in the room. He headed towards it upon getting out of bed. There he wrote "mightbheldar" the strange word he had heard in his dream. The wall was a kind of immense bulletin board, a summary of all the strange experiences he had had since childhood, and that allowed him to contextualize his experiences, at least as far as his visual memory reached. Not knowing for sure if it was a product of the same inherited denial or an internal impulse to preserve sanity, Mae-uhkel had created a complex and extensive map of another world, fantastic, but real for him, as he lived it thía by thía. The strange symbol, which he enclosed in a circle —once again—, was the center of a large diagram composed of myriad notes, names of associated people, places, descriptions of dreams, sketches, and drawings, all corresponding to his supernatural experiences. Interconnected with strands of yarn, he had managed to classify some and

---

4     RB: Remote Broadcast, analogous to TV technology. The receiving device is called BR (Broadcast Receiver)

give them a certain type of relationship; although still full of holes and incomprehensible elements to him, they were an attempt to give coherence and meaning to his strange experiences and thus prove to himself that he was not crazy, or at least remained socially functional.

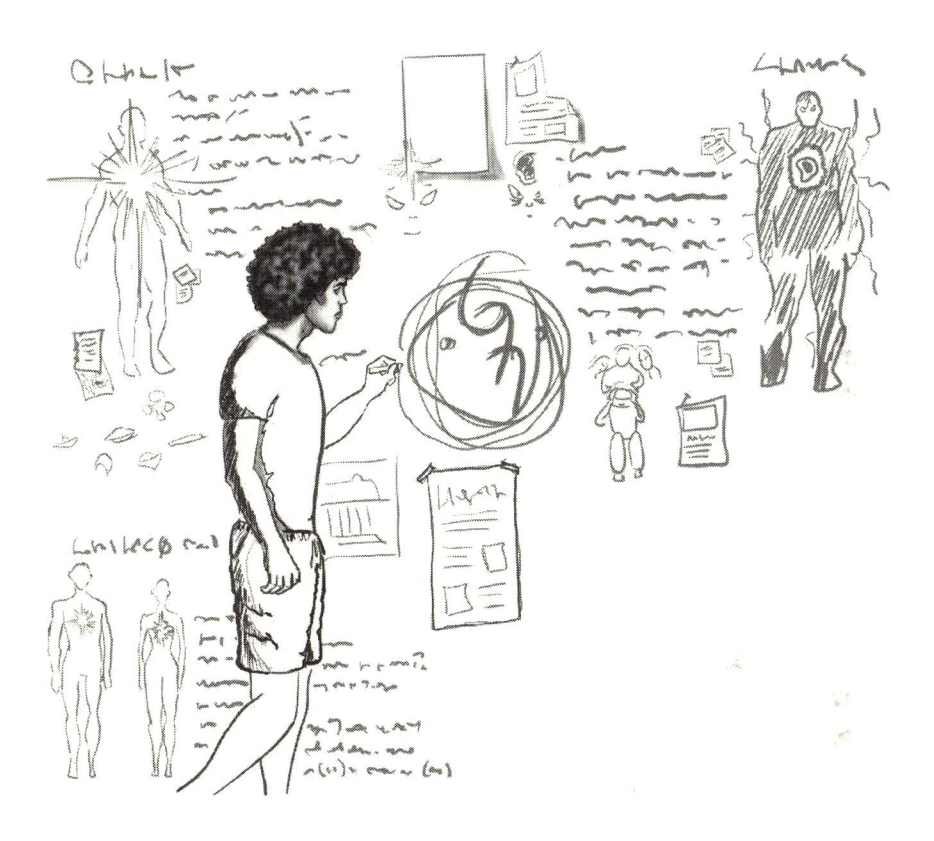

*https://opensea.io/collection/another-world-the-book*

Ready to leave, he took his backpack, his haloguín, and his lunch and gave a loving kiss on the cheek to his mother, who in her haste could only say to him: "...And breakfast?"

"Ah, yes! I'll eat it on the way" he replied, grabbing it as best as he could. He put the paper bag between his teeth and dashed off.

Belonging to the humble class since his father's departure, the young huno and his mother owned nothing, not even a vehicle, so being perfectly on time for work meant flawlessly navigating the entire public transportation network in his town: the Cabletransport, then the Infra, and finally The Communal.

He arrived at the channel a bit early. The director was already there and gave him a nod of approval for being punctual that thía. He greeted him with a wave, marked his arrival, and went to store his things in the locker, put on his uniform, and thus begin his workday. Mae-uhkel worked in the Services and Maintenance Department of TUUS World Network, the main news network of Akuahgrandia, which, thanks to the money, connections, and influence of its shareholders in Hhunuman society, had become an important part of the main Global Communications Network with branches and correspondents all over the planet. His job was hard but ideal for the shy young huno who sought to be as inconspicuous as possible, staying away from people and thus avoiding anyone noticing his problem. Besides, for him, it was temporary, since he was on the verge of graduating from the Major School, and the pay was very good for a part-time job. It had to be, because Mae-uhkel financed his studies and his life, while also supporting his widowed and disabled mother, who tragically lost her left leg in a work accident at the factory where she worked all her life. The company falsely claimed negligence to evade their responsibility in the matter. Thus, her advanced age, her disabled condition, and the tarnished stain on her record became almost insurmountable obstacles to being considered 'eligible' for a decent paying job.

With evening classes in Applied Psychophysics, a field he chose as a way to find scientific explanations for his strange experiences, and rehearsal three nights every quint[5] with the Orchestra where he played the haloguín since he was a child, the young huno's life was quite busy most of the time. He had established as a life rule to respect his vacation time and take it for himself; perhaps that was what had kept him lucid all these cycles.

Halfway through the thía, Mae-uhkel was cleaning the lobby area at the main entrance of the building complex, as usual, isolated from the world, listening to music with his nokó[6], when a young huno looking who looked in a rushed approached him, tapping him on the shoulder and then asked:

"Excuse me, young Huno, could you tell me where the Hunuman Resources area is?"

---

5    A unit of time composed of five thías

6    Electronic communication device.

"Of course, look, continue down this hall wing... - he said, pointing with his hand - turn first to the left and then..."

"No, please!" the hurried Huno interrupted. "Look, this building complex has me very confused. I arrived very early today to make sure I was more than punctual for my interview, and but I got lost in the labyrinth of cubicles and corridors that is this station, which has made me at this point..." he looked at his krono[7] "...Oh Great Gaemo[8]! I am already late. Would you mind if I ask you to take me there? I will be eternally grateful, please!?"

Mae-uhkel could not refuse in the face of the young huno's evident frustration, anguish, and urgency. When they both arrived at the corresponding floor and had taken a couple of turns, Mae-uhkel said:

"Alright, galar[9], follow this hallway..." The huno gestured, urging him to finish the journey with him, but Mae-uhkel continued saying:

"No, no, don't worry, it's not necessary. Look straight ahead, at the end of this hall side, you will find a glass door that leads to a large waiting room; that is the Hunuman Resources Department. There, ask for your interview." He was about to press the elevator button when the huno thanked him for his kindness, placing his hand on his own neck and lowering the head, the common farewell gesture in that part of Hunum, as he hurried away.

Mae-uhkel, intent on returning to his work, nonetheless noticed a peculiar tattoo on the nape of the Huno who was rushing away. It was the symbol!

He immediately felt the urge to follow him, and although he hesitated to do so out of embarrassment, his curiosity was much stronger than his shyness.

Making his way through the crowd, he stepped out of the elevator and hurried to follow him. "Wait, please!" he shouted in an attempt to make him stop and reach him, but the young huno continued his race as if he

---

7    Device to measure time

8    One of the names given to God in Hunum.

9    Galar (male) Galera (female): A term of respect used to address a person who is senior in age, dignity, or position

had not heard him. His arduous effort to catch up was in vain amidst the traffic of people moving in all directions in the busy corridor.

*https://opensea.io/collection/another-world-the-book*

Finally, he reached the room where the Huno was heading, but he was not there. "He must have gone into his meeting" Mae-uhkel thought, yet there too another peculiar scene was unfolding:

"...But I swear I left my documents here last quint. Please, look, I have another copy. If you allow me, I will give them to you, but I beg please, do not discard my application."

Something in the voice speaking caught Mae-uhkel's attention, and he discreetly approached her. It was a beautiful hunuman huna with flawless, fair skin, slender, with silky hair and deep eyes. Apparently, the huna's beauty triggered one of his hallucinations; it was like opening a window to a parallel reality that occurred in synchrony with everyday events. These spasmodic visions came to him at unexpected moments, and Mae-uhkel had no control over them; they came and went without any apparent pattern. However, his learned denial took the reins of this ongoing occurrence, convincing him that he was only daydreaming. He thought that his passion for fantasy and science fiction books and comics had developed in him a – prolific imagination, – a phrase his mother usedall the time to describe him since he was a child when he tried to tell her about his experiences. He had become so prolific that he was capable of creating this entire other world of illusion that unfolded and coexisted with the tangible reality. He chose to think of them as creative dreams rather than resigning himself to accept them as the only legacy his father had left him: a psychotic delirium resulting from the progressive deterioration of his mind. On this occasion, he saw in all those present what he had called –The Core of Fire. – A kind of glow located at the center of all beings, a radiant white light with sparkles of different intensities. He also often heard voices other than his own in his head. He thought of them as the thoughts of others, but deep down, he also knew they might be nothing more than dialogues from a consistent script his disturbed mind created, obeying its subconscious recordings, preconceived criteria, prejudices, and the context in which events unfolded. Perhaps being a writer or screenwriter would have been a better career to pursue. At least then he could then take advantage of his madness, he thought many times; in any case, in this instance, the glow in the chest of the huna who impacted him with her beauty was notably more intense than that of the common hunumans. Next to her glamorous, otherworldly beings that projected and enveloped her in multicolored lights seemed to encourage her in her eagerness to secure that job interview. He didn't know the real reason, perhaps his desire to make sense of his delusion or emulate the stories he read, probably a bit of both, but Mae-uhkel had taken upon himself all these cycles to classify and name all the characters and elements in his hallucinations and capture them on his wall. He called these types of radiant beings, "Gaemas", visible like this hunuman huna and invisible like those accompanying her. They were his favorites because of the sensations of peace, love, compassion, harmony, and beauty he experienced when seeing them, which were very comforting and inspiring.

On the other hand, from the Hunuman Resources employee who was listening to the young huna with a doubtful expression, Mae-uhkel thought he heard a voice saying, "she seems sincere in what she says…" ; but at that very moment, two dark and creepy beings also appeared, part of the young huno's visionary cast, whom he called Tumsas. Wandering shadows of dull colors whose light in the chest looked diminished and faint, they were dark beings, and he had seen them many times at the channel, lurking around the newsrooms and some of the informatists and directors.

These two surrounded the employee, while a dark shadow emerged from their foreheads. The mist enveloped the crown of the huno's head, concentrating and then collapsing in the middle of his forehead. After this happened, he shook his head and replied:

"Hmm no, no, no, I'm sorry, madam! Rules are rules, your papers should be here" he said, tapping the pile of papers on the desk several times; "if they are not, that's not my problem, so, please, you can leave now, I'm very busy" he said with an irritating and haughty voice, and turning around entered his office, closing the door behind him forcefully.

"But how can I explain that I did leave them with your assistant?! "the huna said to the door as it closed right in front of her nose, with a hint of helplessness and disappointment.

*https://opensea.io/collection/another-world-the-book*

Mae-uhkel followed the scene closely while taking steps towards the assistant's desk, initially intending to ask about the strange young huno with the tattoo on his nuke, but in the heat of the moment, he forgot and instead listened to a voice that seemed to come from the desk employee:

"I hope no one finds out!" as she turned her back to pretend, she hadn't noticed what just had happened. Mae-uhkel then thought that she might have been the one who misplaced the applicant's papers in a moment of carelessness. Meanwhile, the young Gaema walked towards the elevator, her head bowed, dropping the folder with her documents into the trash can, and then stood staring out the window, lost in her thoughts and wearing an expression of deep disappointment as she waited for the elevator. Mae-uhkel then felt a desire to help her. Approaching cautiously, he took the folder from the trash can, move toward the huna, and timidly said in a low voice:

"Hey, good thía! Excuse me for intruding, madam. I couldn't help to see what happened just now. I work here" he said, showing her his identification. "Don't be discouraged. I'm a good friend of Galera Rúbik, who is the director of Hunuman Resources and supervisor of the guy who you just talked a moment ago. I took the liberty of retrieving this from the trash" he said, showing her the documents. "If you like, I can get them to her."

"Oh! Really? That would be wonderful, thank you so much" the young huna replied with a wide smile, visibly injected with hope and feeling deep gratitude towards this stranger who surprisingly offered to help, then she added:

"I'm Nissa, Nissa Berdat - she extended her hand." Pleased to meet you, Galar...

"Mae-uhkel, Mae-uhkel Granahoi, but don't call me galar, I might even be younger than you."

"Well, then don't be formal with me either; call me Nissa"

"Alright, Nissa, I got your papers; you can go in peace"

"Wow, Mae-uhkel, I really don't know how to thank you. Can I ask why you're doing this?"

"I don't know, I would say I just feel like it" (hidden his real motivation) "and by the way, thank you for letting me help you and not freaking out with a stranger approaching. I hope we see each other again when galera Berdat start working here" he said, giving her a wink.

"Please, the pleasure and luck were mine, and remember, 'Nissa', we agreed no more formalities... Goodbye, Mae-uhkel, and thank you so much again" Nissa replied as she entered the elevator. Both had felt a mutual attraction, not a typical huno-huna attraction, but a sense of mutual camaraderie, as if they already knew each other.

In the afternoon, Mae-uhkel headed to the office of Galera Rúbik. Despite his hermit-like nature, Mae-uhkel was kind, attentive, and loving with people, which made him appreciated by most of the staff at the plant.

"Good thía, Galera Rúbik! How are you?" greeted Mae-uhkel.

"Hello, 'Mae-uhkely,'" she said affectionately "good thía to you too. Did you have some Shazaá?" she asked kindly, while serving herself from the Shazaatera.

"No, thank you, I don't drink Shazaá" he said with a smile, remembering once seeing a tiny Bham-yi next to galera Rúbik. These curious creatures from his other world represented for him the habits, customs, and even vices of people. With a viscous and sticky appearance, their shapes and sizes were multiple, generally related to the energy they seemed to feed on through energetic threads attached to their host. In this case, the Bham-yi of galera absorbed energy from her each time she took a sip of the stimulating drink.

https://opensea.io/collection/another-world-the-book

"Galera Rúbik, I came for a couple of things, a question, and a small favor..."

"Whatever you want, dear. Tell me, how can I help you?" reply the huna.

"Well, two things, first I want to ask about a huno who was interviewed earlier today, he was a..."

"But wait Mae-uhkel" she interrupted his discourse "today is not an interview thía, dear."

"Oh, but he told me he had an appointment."

"He must have been confused about the thía; today the entire department, including myself, is very busy organizing and scheduling the new round of interviews for this season. I don't think anyone would have had time to attend to him today."

Puzzled, Mae-uhkel wondered if it was another creation of his mind. Some were difficult to distinguish from reality either because they didn't have a fantastical character or because they didn't involve others. Then he continued: "I understand, I must have misunderstood" he said, trying to brush the topic under the carpet, then continued "the other matter that brings me here, Galera Rubik, is this look" he said, handing her Nissa's folder. "She is a good friend of mine and my family. Apparently, she left her papers downstairs at the reception office, but they got lost. I was wondering if it would be too much trouble for you to receive them."

"Of course, Mae-uhkelín, there's no problem at all. Besides, if she comes recommended by you, she must be an excellent worker." The galera took the folder without looking at it and placed it in the pile with the rest of the applicants. "Thank you very much, Galera Rúbik, for the favor and the compliment... and one more thing, please don't say anything to Galar Ban Dinhú. He had already rejected her, but he was the one who lost the papers. Actually, I think it might have been a mix-up by the assistant."

"Surely...!" she said, as if recognizing a recurrent attitude in the mentioned employee. "Don't worry, I'll tell him that I took them from her desk."

"Oh, that would be great! Thank you so much again!"

"It's nothing, Mae-uhkel. Have a good thía!"

"You too."

The image of Nissa her retinue of Light remained in Mae-uhkel's mind for the rest of the thía, and upon arriving home that evening, he noted her name on his wall as a – Visible Gaema, – then went to sleep. He was satisfied to have been able to help her. Now, he only asked the Great Gaemo that her interview would be successful.

---

Several quints passed, and one morning at home, Nissa turned on the BR while preparing her breakfast.

"...We need more investments and fewer taxes. More jobs, more production. Vote so we can keep moving forward, keep up the good pace. Vote for Munai [10] Sekk Ragner, Our Magnhuno!"

Nissa made a face of disgust and disapproval...

"Coming up in the main worldwide BR news program morning edition... To know what's happening around the globe, only here on TUUS World Network... Headlines: The Chancellor of Akuahgrandia meets today in Freites with counterparts from Z-suní and Deilgohu in search of peace. A series of repeated earthquakes shakes the coasts of Hulkores. Religious conflicts in Facullá continue, leaving dozens dead and hundreds injured. In the world of entertainment, media magnate Drakur Zoren Zics suffered a new crisis; health professionals recommend patience to his family and loved ones, and in sports..."

"Galek?" she thought to herself, recognizing one of the magnate's sons in the images where he was being interviewed. "Of course, Galek 'Zoren Zic'! Wow! I never even considered that he could be related to 'Drakur Zoren Zic...'" she said emphatically "...let alone his son."

Nissa was a young informatist[11] with a combative character but also with great hunuman sensitivity. Therefore, after a thoughtful pause, she felt sympathy for the situation of her former classmate at the Major School and decided to contact him to offer support; she thought to herself:

"Poor thing, it must be very hard. If it were my dad in that situation,

---

10  Title for those who achieved the highest academic degree.
11  Hunuman profession that involves the acquisition, processing, interpretation, and dissemination of information through any written, oral, visual, or graphic medium.

I'd be devastated... Who might have his nokode? Barhana Quy, yes, she was always with him at the Major School." She took her nokó and dialed

"Hello, Barhana? Hi, it's Nissa! Yes, all good, thank you. Do you happen to have Galek's nokode?" She paused and waited. "Great! Tell me." She noted it in her nokó. "It's just that I just found out about galar Drakur's condition, and I wanted to call to offer my help. He must be going through a tough time. Thanks a million, Barhana, goodbye." She ended the call and immediately dialed again. "Yes, good afternoon, am I speaking with Galek?... Hi Galek, it's me, Nissa, Nissa Berdat from the Major School, friend of Barhana."

On the other end of the nokó, the call from Nissa surprised and even excited Galek, who remembered her perfectly from the Department of Public Communication at the Major School where they both studied. Although they had spoken little, they felt a great affinity for each other, and Nissa's beauty was not easy to forget:

"Hello, Nissa, what a surprise!"

"Yes, I heard about your father and wanted to tell you how sorry I am. I would also like to offer my help in any way you think I can be of assistance. My father is a Munai Health Specialist at the Main Center in Akuahgrandia. It's not his area of expertise, but he has helped many people with various ailments outside his field to heal by implementing changes in their nutrition and lifestyles" she paused because she found her innocent comment amusing and added: "I understand that you must have your super team of professionals, but you know, second opinions or unconventional methods are always good" she said, somewhat justifying her naive suggestion, then added: "...and of course, if you need someone to talk to..." she concluded, feeling already embarrassed by Galek's silence, who remained only listening attentively.

"Thank you very much, Nissa" he replied, "but I honestly don't think my family would lean towards that option." Nissa blushed and almost regretted calling. "However,..." Galek continued "...the offer about talking to someone does interest me..." Nissa breathed a sigh of relief, "it's true, although it might seem unbelievable, it's in these moments that true friends appear; most people only come close when you're partying. I really appreciate it. The truth is, a lot has happened, and I haven't had time to assimilate everything. I've saved your nokode; is this the right one?"

"Yes."

"Definitely I will call you soon. You offered your help, so now I'll bother you" he joked, breaking the initial tension.

"It won't be a bother at all; I'll be here when you need me. Let's talk, and I hope everything goes well. Goodbye!"

"Okay, thanks, but not goodbye, better to say see you soon!" he emphasized, showing genuine interest. After ending the call, Nissa chuckled at herself for considering her comment about her father's services ridiculous, mimicking herself in offering them. Then she thought that, fortunately, it seemed like her call had been well-received after all. She then became thoughtful and smiled compassionately. "He sounded calm. He must be a very strong person... even with everything that's going on, he doesn't lose his sympathy and calm" she thought.

---

Near the TUUS building, a leaflet distributor walked carelessly when he was suddenly struck with the urge check his nokó, as if prompted by someone else. The young huno put the stack of leaflets aside to do so, and the particularly strong wind that afternoon blew several of them away, to which the boy reacted with surprise and displeasure. Grumbling, he picked up what he could, putting them back in his stack to continue his route. Later, at the end of the thía, Mae-uhkel was leaving the channel on his way to the Major School, and one of the leaflets left behind by the distributor flew to his feet. Mae-uhkel picked it up and read:

*"DO YOU WONDER WHAT'S HAPPENING TO YOU? COME AND DISCOVER YOUR DESTINY, The Great Izora, The Mystic. She will see what you cannot and tell you what you want to know."*

He read the leaflet, which was interspersed with images of mysterious tarot cards, candles, and strange symbols. He looked at the address; it was nearby where he was, he checked his krono and had ample time before his first class, so he decided to go see Izora. Perhaps she could help him understand and overcome all those strange things that were happening to him. He had already tried with the cleric of his community, but several times he had been told that these were not matters of Gaemo and that he should seek professional help. Still, Mae-uhkel refused to turn to the

Munaies because he didn't want to resign himself to accepting that he was crazy, although he often wondered if it might be true.

He arrived at the place. It was a dark room filled with candles, heads of stuffed animals, strange potions hanging from doors and walls, and a strong smell of incense enveloping the entire atmosphere. Amulets hanging, small religious statues of beings, half hunuman, half animal, and others showing immense suffering on their faces were the master stroke of the gloomy scene, worthy of a mournful horror novel. A pale-skinned huna with somewhat exaggerated makeup and too much perfume, sitting behind a desk, asked him:

*https://opensea.io/collection/another-world-the-book*

"Yes? At your service. Are you here for a card reading, palm reading, or Shazaá reading?"

"No, actually, I came to see Galera Izora for."

" 'The Great Izora' " the peculiar assistant interrupted him, raising her index finger and correcting him.

"Well, yes, Galera Great Izora…"

"It's ghori[12] debos[13], and it must be paid here in advance. Wait a

---
12   Hunuman number
13   Akuahgrandian currency

moment" she said as she stood up and crossed the curtain leading to the adjoining room when at the same time a couple of women came out of the room, one crying on the other's shoulder.

Inside the room, the assistant was about to tell the Mystic about the client outside but she made her stop with a rude gesture, she was receiving a mystical message right in that moment.

"The mortal who is about to enter seeking for your holy guidance is called Mae-uhkel. He has a very severe mental illness which will become more and more disturbing with time and comes for advice from your vast wisdom, oh great Izora! He must understand that his mind is broken, is trying to escape from this world. Making accept that real life is in the real world. Help him with your sapience Great Master."

Then Izora said with a solemn voice to the reverent assistant:

" I know, let him in"

The attendant came out and seating down said:

"The Great Izora is ready for you, but you need to pay first."

"Alright, sure" Mae-uhkel replied as he took the payment from his pouch "though it seems a bit expensive just to chat for a while."

The assistant's twisted smile showed mockery at the young huno's naivety, who obviously, in her eyes, failed to understand the powers of – The Mystic. – Right before crossing the curtain. Mae-uhkel felt chills followed by a sensation he had felt before, a feeling of discomfort and alertness. This awakened his vision. He saw what appeared to be ordinary hunumans leaving the room through the walls, but they were invisible. Mae-uhkel was used to this because he had seen them many times before, walking indifferently among crowds, seemingly unaware that they were invisible to others. Some, aware of their invisibility, wandered around, some indifferent, others confused, and some even trying to communicate with ordinary hunumans making them aware of their presence. Mae-uhkel wasn't sure if they existed beyond his head and had trained himself not to pay attention to them. Upon entering, two of these ordinary invisibles remained in the room. Their expressions were tormented, confused, and anguished, and the glow in their hearts was small, making their color seem to be fading, turning brownish. Izora, on the other hand, was a brown-skinned huna dressed extravagantly, with a dozen necklaces hanging from her neck, hands full of bracelets and rings, and a veil on her head that perfectly completed the curious character. But what really struck him was seeing her accompanied by two brown Tumsas who laughed mockingly and a Bham-yi floating beside her. It seemed that the Tumsas were mocking poor Izora, who remained oblivious and immovable, sitting in front of her crystal ball. Their laughs and taunts contrasted with the seriousness of – The Mystic, – who smoked a fragrant substance from a long straw connected to a smoking device. These Tumsas were less gloomy and more sarcastic. The Bham-yi fed off her each time she took the thin pipe to her mouth. Then he saw how two of the Tumsas whispered to each other, after which one laughed, cleared his throat to mimic a deeper and more mysterious voice, and said into her ear:

"This is Mae-uhkel oh Great Izora!" Then he moved away, continuing to laugh heartily with the others.

"You're Mae-uhkel, right?" inquired Izora, pointing at him with her finger, intending to surprise him with her divination, and she succeeded…

*https://opensea.io/collection/another-world-the-book*

...But not because of the divination itself, but for Mae-uhkel, it was a milestone. An interesting indication that what happened on an invisible level was somehow also perceived by Izora... A hint that his visions were not just in his head... It seemed that these Tumsas enjoyed posing as wise spirits and confusing the unwary who sought answers to their problems in the unseen through the clairvoyant. Mae-uhkel silently thanked her, but realizing that those Tumsas were invisible even to her, who apparently could only hear them. He looked at her with compassion, saying, "I think you need more help than I do, thank you anyway!" He immediately left; a little disappointed at not having obtained answers from the Mystic, he took his debos, still warm and crumpled from being in his pouch just moments before, took a few steps towards the exit under the puzzled gaze of the assistant; but then he reconsidered, turned around, and , before leaving, he placed them back on the table as a silent token of gratitude for what Izora had unknowingly shown him. He had seen all he needed to see from 'The Mystic'.

After these events, his mood changed; the possibility that his visions might be real excited him. That evening, after leaving the Major School and during his rehearsal, he played the haloguín like never before, and in the climactic stages of the pieces, the segments that excited him the most; he saw multiple colors emanating from his haloguín, the rest of the instruments, and even the musicians. He even saw beautiful Gaemas dancing and seeming to enjoy the music as much or more than he did.

Although this was normal for Mae-uhkel and he had never told anyone but his notebook, his wall, and a little to his mother when he was a child, that evening he looked at everything with different eyes. Could such splendid beings truly exist? The idea gave him goosebumps, but immediately the image of his father, asserting that everything he saw was true, transformed his expression instantly. The way he was treated by the hospital staff, their jeers, and the demeaning and contemptuous way they humored him were the antidote to his small doses of hope. Had he also imagined all that? The Mystic, her office, and her reaction?

https://opensea.io/collection/another-world-the-book

At the same time, on the other side of the planet in the country of Lukón, there was Masaru Takashi, a Munai in physical chemistry, who had dedicated the last cycles of his life to the development of Eco Synthesis[14]. This was a brave decision for several reasons: first, it was a territory reserved for physics, which was not his main field, and second, he risked not being taken seriously by members of the world's scientific academy, who viewed the topic with great skepticism, almost esoteric, due to past events. However, Masaru truly believed it was possible and saw it as a solution to the global energy problem, as it was a clean and cheap source. A brilliant scientist, tall, with a humble but elegant appearance and grey hair that showed a life dedicated to study, he was also a boehara[15] at the National Major School of Shunsuke, a great hunumanist and lover of science, which he conceived as a way to understand nature. In his laboratory, Masaru received a call:

"Good morning, Main Laboratory!"

"Good morning! is this Munai Takashi?" a deep voice inquired.

"Yes, speaking."

*https://opensea.io/collection/another-world-the-book*

---

14    Physical chemistry process, similar to cold fusion.

15    Chair Professor

"Greetings, Munai! This is Kohtaro Yu from the Magnhunial Office of the Nation."

"Oh, yes, tell me, Galar Yu, how can I be of service?"

"I regret having to contact you under these circumstances, Munai, but it is my duty to inform you that the government has been forced to make the decision to... suspend the financial support for your research."

"Excuse me, What? What are you saying? I don't understand." He sat down in his chair, surprised and incredulous.

"I am not allowed to give any arguments, Munai. All I can say is that under the current tense international circumstances, your project has been defined as 'Non-Priority'..."

"That makes no sense!" the Munai retorted, still shocked and confused. "How? Just recently I spoke with the Magnhuno in person, and he expressed his appreciation for our team's work. Our research is on the right track and would be part of the solution...".

"...Non-priority," his interlocutor interrupted. "The growing tensions between our allies and Deilgohu force us to adjust the budget and immediately divert those resources to military investment and defense..."

"Even more so then!" he said, responding to what he considered an absurd argument. "The success of our work would be the end of the conflict. The main reason for the conflict is energy..."

"Munai, excuse me," his interlocutor interrupted again, this time with a louder tone and showing contempt. "I am not authorized to extend this conversation; these are the orders; I can't speak any further. Have a good afternoon, Munai!" he said, ending the call.

"Excuse me, Galar Yu, but those arguments... Hello! Hello?... Damn!" he exclaimed as he hung up the nokó. Sitting in his office, utterly troubled, Masaru remained thoughtful for a few moments. His lost gaze was a sign of how bewildered he was by the unexpected decision and the arguments used to justify it. He looked for nokó numbers of acquaintances who might explain what happened and help him continue financing the project. He spoke with the few who answered his call, but to no avail; it was as if everyone had agreed not to inform him or offer support. After several failed attempts, he gave up, realizing they were in vain. Defeated, he stood up, left his office, and addressed his team with the bad news.

"Everyone, please stop what you're doing; I need your full attention." The whole team gathered around the Munai, who said with a look of clear disappointment, "I regret to inform you that the government is unable to continue financing our research, and we have no one else..." Everyone looked at each other, surprised and confused. After a silence, some began to murmur comments, and others threw questions into the air: "What does this mean? Why? It's impossible!" The Munai continued. "...I just received the news... I will look for ways to continue our work. However, please prepare a report on the current status of your processes. Thank you all for your dedication and ethic over these cycles. It was an honor for me to work alongside such a valuable team." He addressed each one with a hug, expressing his individual gratitude and emphasizing each one's respective contribution. Then he returned to his office and began to pack up his belongings. When he was putting away the photos from his desk, he saw a photo of his daughter Etzuko, took it in his hands, kissed it, and held it to his chest. Etzuko had been in Akuahgrandia for... "Wow, already ten cycles." He though. It seemed like yesterday when he saw her off at the airport. She had been sent as the deputy director of the Lukón embassy in that country and he hadn't seen her since. The immense distance between countries located at opposite poles of Hunum, along with his dedication to his research and busy routine at the Major School, had not given Masaru a chance to host her at his home, let alone travel to Akuahgrandia. He missed her so much, and only now, forced to pause his hectic schedule, did he realize how much he had neglected his relationship with his beloved daughter. At that moment, he closed his eyes for a few moments and apparently felt a strong impulse that led him to say, "Ah, and why not now?" He quickly got up, finished storing his belongings, and left; he seemed to have made an important decision. On his way home, he took out his nokó:

"Good afternoon, I would like to book a flight to Akuahgrandia, please... No, one-way only..."

# CHAPTER 2

## SEARCHING FOR ANSWERS IS AN INSIDE JOB

The thía after talking with his supervisor and having finished the term at the Major School, Mae-uhkel was officially on vacation from all his regular activities. On his way back home, he got off the CT and, heading towards the Infra near an alley, he encountered a completely unusual and unexpected situation. A couple of hunos were shouting insults at each other from a distance. He tried to ignore them and continue on his way, but in the blink of an eye, what seemed like a simple argument suddenly turned into a street gang fight, trapping him in the middle of it. The adrenaline of the moment once again awakened the young huno's visions, and he ran to hide in a corner. He saw how the involved parties appeared to be influenced by Tumsas. An elderly huna in a corner prayed for the fight to stop, and her calls were answered by some Gaemas. Others from the Light faction were there too, but remained beside each of those fighting, patiently static, attentive to intervene but without doing so. It seemed they were waiting for a call from the involved parties, who were instead intoxicated in their slander, feeding more and more to the Bham-yis of Hatred and Discord. The luminous ones who answered the elder huna's call were trying to stop the dark ones. Although one of them seemed able to neutralize several of their opponents, they were much fewer in number and, besides, the shadowy ones seemed to be strengthened by the attitudes, screams, and blows of the gangsters.

*https://opensea.io/collection/another-world-the-book*

When members of both gangs pulled out firearms, and one of them shot other, Mae-uhkel took advantage of the chaos to slip away, running towards the Infra station. He stumbled onto the platform and boarded the Infra car, sitting down frightened, panting and hugging his bag.

During the train ride, after calming down a little, Mae-uhkel replayed in his head the events he had just experienced. Visibly shaken, he wondered:

"What good is everything I can see if I can't do anything with it...?" The young huno lamented, hitting his head against the window of the coach, his hands still trembling. Startled and trembling, he felt a great frustration mixed with fear and helplessness caused by the dangerous situation he had been involved in. This mental and emotional state of Mae-uhkel opened the door for an idea to sneak into his mind:

"Why not end this once and for all?... It's simple... He ended everything easily... yes, in a flash of a moment and the torment is over!" He got the thought in his head but almost immediately said to himself:

"No, no, how can I even think that... I'm not a coward like him; I can't leave my mother alone as he did." he said, taking his damaged nokó to search for information about his condition in a desperate attempt to find answers, as he had done many times before, but as always, he found nothing concrete. On the contrary, he felt more confused the more he searched. For science, it was schizophrenia, for religion, a curse. Both answers only sank him deeper into despair. Upon leaving the Infra, he stopped at the oratory in front of the Cable-T station, entered, knelt as was customary in his religion, looked up at the kulka[16], and after sobbing for a few moments with his eyes filled with tears fixed on the statue of the martyr hanging in front of him, he implored:

https://opensea.io/collection/another-world-the-book

"Please help me, beloved daughter of Gaemo!... Am I cursed, or what do you want from me? Why now, when I would like to see, do I see nothing?" he asked. "Have I lost my sanity? No... That witch heard them too, I know she heard them... so they were there, right?... Oh my Galera, if they are really visions, there should be a reason, tell me; otherwise, I don't want them anymore..." he said, crying. Images of his father came to his head repeatedly, memories of his childhood with him, and of the visits that he and his mother made to him in the thías leading up to his tragedy.

---

16  Kulka: Instrument of torture and execution used in ancient times in Hunum (similar to the Earthly gallows). For the religion that dominated in that region of the planet, the Kulka was, paradoxically, adored and venerated as a holy symbol, because it was where their Messiah was executed, giving her life for them.

"No, I'm not crazy like him... I'm not crazy like him... that witch was real... give me understanding, please...!" he cried out, with the last breath that his deep lament had left in his lungs. Looking down, he remained dejected and absorbed, his poor spirit already defeated by what was undoubtedly too much for a single individual to bear. An overwhelming task to live and function on the edge of two realities, both equally intense and impactful, and without the assurance that one of them even truly existed beyond his imagination. Kneeling at the feet of the wooden Messiah, he sobbed. After a while, he dried his tears, stood up, and walked out of the building.

He arrived at the neighborhood where he lived, strangely empty at that time of the thía, where only a stray drapo[17] in the middle of the park could be seen scratching and howling at the rising Dahna behind the buildings. He took the elevator to his apartment floor and lay back, exhausted more from mental torment than physical fatigue. The elevator suddenly stopped and opened a couple of floors before his destination, then turned off as if the electricity had been cut.

"Fantastic!" he exclaimed sarcastically and stubbornly. He tried persistently but unsuccessfully to press the button for his floor, which obviously did not work. Disappointed and downcast, almost dragging his feet, he left the elevator and headed to the stairs to climb to his apartment. As he trudged along, almost reaching his floor, his attention was drawn to strange lights escaping through the cracks framing the door of the apartment right in front of the stairs.

His dismay turned into curiosity as he approached the entrance of the dwelling. What could that be? "Another vision?" he thought warily. He noticed that the numberplate of the flat was not the standard one, horizontally arranged, used in the rest of the building, this one was vertical. Maybe the owners lost the original and made their own by hand, but this unit had too many strange things about it.

---

17   Hunuman animal popularly used as pet

*https://opensea.io/collection/another-world-the-book*

As he tried to place his ear against the door of the mysterious apartment to find out the source of the light show, he almost fell over a sweet old huna who opened the door just at that moment.

*https://opensea.io/collection/another-world-the-book*

"Good evening, Mae-uhkel. Were you looking for something?" the kindly old huna asked him.

Surprised and somewhat embarrassed, Mae-uhkel stammered: "Uhh, no, sorry!... but do you know me?"

"Yes, you're Mae-uhkel, the son of Galera Granahoi from upstairs. I've known you all your life; your mother came to this building many cycles ago when you were just a little one, and look at you now, all grown up... How the time flies!"

"Yes, that's right, Galera..." he said, dragging out the last vowel, hoping the huna would finish the sentence and trying to peek inside the apartment from which such strange lights had been emerging just moments before, but noticing nothing out of the ordinary.

"Leyhana, my name is Leyhana."

"A pleasure meeting you, Galera Leyhana, I had never seen you before. Excuse me, but I got the wrong apartment! I was distracted and thought it was mine, since it's just a couple of floors above yours. The elevator stopped here without me intending it to and..."

"Are you sure you got it wrong?" she interrupted sweetly. "You seem a bit anxious, like you're looking for something..." noticing the poorly disguised insistence of Mae-uhkel on look at the interior of her house.

"Yes! Actually, no, sorry!" he stammered, embarrassed, knowing he was caught in his snooping.

"No, don't worry, it's no problem then, good night!" said the senior huna to smooth over the young huno's obvious embarrassment and confusion. As he hung his head and turned to leave, she was about to close her door but before saying goodbye she added "just in case you are actually looking for something… we are all always looking for something..." she said thoughtfully "remember to look first – inside – rather than – outside – ... ALWAYS the answers we seek are no further than our own heart…" she said with a deep sight before finishing with a motherly "Good night, my child!" finally closing her door for good now.

The phrase resonated like a bell in the young huno's mind as he went home, pondering the uncannily opportune words spoken by his strange neighbor.

Shunsuke International Airport was crowded with people that thía, and Masaru was nervous about missing his flight due to the long line. Nervously, he fidgeted with his printed ticket in his hands. Suddenly, an airline employee stood at one of the empty counters adjacent to his line and gestured for him to come over. At first, Masaru didn't understand that the huna's gestures were directed at him. Turning in all directions to see who she was talking to; the employee insisted and called him by his last name:

"Galar Takashi!"

*https://opensea.io/collection/another-world-the-book*

"Yes… excuse me, why are you taking me out of the line?"

"For seniority, my galar."

"Oh…" The kind employee was wearing a strange symbol around her neck. Coincidentally, it was the same one that Mae-uhkel often saw. After checking his documents, she informed him: "We've upgraded you to Premier class for your loyalty to our company."

"That's curious, I've only flown with you maybe a couple of times." The employee smiled and replied: "Sometimes the system grants these upgrades randomly as well to encourage our customers."

"Oh, then lucky me! at least on this" said the Munai with a smile on his face.

"Here's your documents and your boarding pass. Have a good trip Munai…"

Masaru took it and went to inform an elderly couple who were three spots behind him to go to the counter the young huna had manned…

"Excuse me, you can go to the counter where the young huna who helped, she is taking care of seniors…" When he turned to point them in the right direction, he realized the kind employee was no longer there and the counter was closed. "Oh, sorry, she was just there a moment ago. Maybe she'll be back shortly. Keep an eye out" was all he could tell them.

The flight proceeded normally, and as they were about to land in Akuahgrandia…

"…It would be a revolution in energy sources. Look, a small cube of fuel like this could satisfy the energy needs of an entire building for several cycles or a family for a lifetime. Moreover, Eco Synthesis energy not only doesn't pollute and is inexhaustible, but it's also much cheaper to obtain. Imagine free energy! All nations and villages around the world, no matter how remote, could have their own generating plants, and we could even think of vehicles powered by free fuel, portable generators, inexhaustible nanomic batteries, non-stop air and sea travel, even interplanetary trips…"

Masaru was explaining to his seatmate on the plane, just about to land at the Akuahgrandia capital's airport. Although Masaru spoke the language of Akuahgrandia and four others fluently, his interlocutor was an elderly huna who didn't understand a word of what he was saying but was greatly amused by the deep passion and friendliness with which the Munai explained his theories. However, the airline's upgrade to Premier class had coincidentally seated him behind Kelia Zaver, the Akuahgrandian Magnhunial candidate, who was returning from diplomatic duties in Lukón.

*https://opensea.io/collection/another-world-the-book*

"It would be the end of hunger, wars, hegemonic dominance she was about to turn and say something, however, her thoughts were interrupted by the flight attendant:

"Nomocat[18], please excuse me, but you need to turn everything off; we are about to land."

"Oh, I'm sorry, yes, of course" said Kelia, hurrying to finish what she was doing and gather her belongings in preparation for the descent.

Once outside the arrival terminal, Masaru placed all his luggage in the transport, deciding at the last minute to visit his daughter before going to his final lodging.

"To the Lukón mission, please."

At the embassy, Etzuko was working as usual:

"Yes, please send these papers to the foundation and make an appointment with the people from HITUSHI for this afternoon... Thank you, Galar Natzuke."

---

18    Diplomatic title in Akhuagrandia and other countries in Hunum who represent the interests of the people and is responsible for making, debating, and voting on laws, and also overseeing the actions of the other members of the government.

"Madame Takashi, you are requested at the entrance."

"Oh no, I can't right now, Miyú! Just please, whoever it is, take their names and nokodes, and I'll contact them as soon as I can" she said hesitantly while sorting some papers in her hands with hurry.

"I'm sorry, Madame Takashi, but the galar says he's your father..."

"My father?!" Etzuko stopped in her tracks, confused. She paused, diverting her path to head towards the reception, handed the papers she had in her hand to her assistant, and hurried to the entrance to see what it was about. It couldn't be her father; he wouldn't have time to come to Akuahgrandia, let alone do so without telling her. Upon reaching the reception, she couldn't believe her eyes, which immediately filled with tears upon seeing him standing there with his briefcase slung over his shoulder, exactly as she remembered the thía he said goodbye ten cycles ago. It was such an utterly surprise that she couldn´t help but run to hug him tightly.

"Dad?!... Daddy!!! But what are you doing here? How?... And your experiments, your laboratory, the Major School?"

"Hello, my Etzi" they hug for seconds that seamed eternal, equivalent to so many cycles without each other, then he said "Well, it's a very long story; I just wanted to see you and personally tell you that I´m here..".

"And where were you planning to stay?"

"Oh, a very good place on the outskirts of the city."

"Well, absolutely not, really? how can it be, look," she took a pen and a small notebook from the reception desk, "this is my address... and these..." she put her hand in her jacket pocket and handed him a bunch of keys "are the keys to the house, please go and wait for me this afternoon, make yourself comfortable. There are two bedrooms upstairs, choose whichever you like, sorry for the mess, okay? But well, I got something from you..." she joked, "and I don't want a 'no' for an answer; by the way, wait..." she took out her nokó and dialed. "Hello Galar Natzuke, have you made the appointment with HITUSHI crew? Good, I will be busy this afternoon, it'll be better for tomorrow mid- morning please... because this dahna will be for long talking" she said, smiling softly to her father and covering the nokó. "Yes, yes galar Natzuke I know I said it was a priority but I just got a private matter I need to take care of immediately, thank you, yes, don't worry I'll catch up, see you later." She hanged up... "All set! So, see you this afternoon?"

"Oh, but how can I say no to you?!" her father replied, happy to see his Etzi again. They hugged each other again and said goodbye until the end of the afternoon, where they would surely spend a lot of time rekindling a father-daughter relationship that had been frozen for ten long and busy cycles.

---

Nissa's nokó rang a couple of times before she answered it:

"Hello?"

"Nissa? Hi, it's me, Galek... I see you didn't save my nokode..."

"Hello, Galek!" she said, laughing and then a bit embarrassed "...Very observant! Well, you are right, that thía I dialed directly and then forgot to save it, but I'm glad you decided to call back... Is everything okay?"

"Yes… well…no changes really but tell me, do you think we could meet today? Maybe at the end of the thía, or are you busy?"

"No, I've got nothing going on tonight, so sure, but where?"

"I don't know, I thought we could hang around, talk for a while and have a drink. What do you think?"

"Sounds good to me, where do we meet?"

"Well I could come to your place, if that is okay with you?"

"Oh yes, that's fine, thank you! … take down my address…" Galek noted her address and started making arrangements.

A little later than planned, he arrived at Nissa's house, got out of the vehicle, and knocked on the door:

"Come in and have a seat, I'm almost ready." He heard Nissa's voice from inside. "Can you give me a moment?"

"Of course, take your time… I'm sure the restaurant won't move from there…" They both laughed, and Galek sat down in the living room.

*https://opensea.io/collection/another-world-the-book*

It was a beautifully decorated space in a minimalist style, not too small or too large, comfortable and spacious enough for Nissa, who had lived there alone since her past times at the Major School. Coming from a well-off family in the province of Akuahgrandia, they had bought her this residence so she could study at the National Major School in the country's capital. The large number of books, all well-worn from use, in the bookshelf were mostly on Public Communication, but also included politics, philosophy, art, biographies of great historic leaders, history, and even some hard science fiction, indicating that Nissa was an avid reader and not an ordinary girl; indeed, she never had been. From a young age, she was very bright, a lover of knowledge, and rebellious against the established order. Outspoken, what she did not understand or agree with, she openly expressed. At the Major School, she was part of the Student Core, defending the rights of her fellow students and the institution itself against the excesses of the State or other institutions. She was an eternal seeker and defender of truth and equity. That's why she studied journalism, to seek the truth of facts and disseminate information as objectively and truthfully as possible even in the toughest circumstances.

Meanwhile, Galek was a handsome, well-built young huno, belonging to the race that held supremacy in Hunum. Tall, with straight, dark hair, but cut short in the style of the wealthy class he belonged to, though this did not matter much to him. His straightforward character and unpretentious behavior made him stand out in a family among the few who together held absolute power and wealth in a country where the elites governed and controlled society, and even more so from his father, known as The Media Magnate, who always wanted his son to follow in his footsteps as a great businessman. Being the only son, he was the one expected to take on the role in his father's absence, but Galek did not desire that role. He was a person completely detached from material things despite having everything since childhood. Growing up immersed in the world of audiovisual news, he decided to study Public Communication, against his father's will and despite his multiple attempts to introduce him to business since he was a teenager. Due to the magnate's delicate health, the handsome young huno now found himself at a crossroads: he had to take care of the family empire's interests and lead it in the absence of his father, who was on the brink of death, or follow his inclination and continue his life as a normal hunuman. It was a moment of decision in Galek's life where on one side were everybody's expectations and on the other, his autonomy and happiness.

"Ready?"

"Yes, let's go."

They spent the afternoon immersed in conversation, gradually peeling back the layers of one another's personalities. The chemistry between them was undeniable, a magnetic pull that became more apparent with every shared smile and lingering glance. Galek took the opportunity to cathartically share his situation with Nissa. They talked about their childhoods and their ages at the Major School. After a while sharing, Galek became curious about why Nissa wasn't currently working. He asked her, and she explained:

"Until very recently, I worked at a regional RB channel near the Major School. With the change in regional authorities, there was also a change in staff. Those of us who were there were replaced by people from the new government. They told us: 'Anyone who wants to keep their job must adapt to the fact that there will be a change in focus here.' That was reason enough for me to leave, and so I did…"

"But… aren't you looking for a job?"

"Of course, I have submitted my applications to several RB channels and am waiting."

"But what about my family´s?"

"TUUS? Not yet" she answered hesitantly. Nissa thought about hiding the incident she had experienced a few quints ago. Due to her temperament and convictions, she did not want Galek to do anything to help her get a job at the channel. However, she also didn't want to lie to him, so she decided to be fully honest.

"Well, actually, yes..."

"Why did you say no?"

"Because I don't want you to even think that I'm seeking your help, and much less that you do anything to help me."

"Please promise me you won't!"

"Hmm, to be honest, I don't know, Nissa. You seem to me like a sincere person a passionate professional, with a lot of ethics. That's not common at my father's channel. I think your presence on the staff could change some things. I know you want to achieve things on your own, and that's commendable, but believe me, if I don't intervene, they won't let you in. The channel's line is tough, and when they see your resume as a somewhat liberal fighter and an informatist who wants to tell a truth different from theirs and against their interests, they won't allow it. Let me help you, take it as you doing me a favor, ha ha! Once inside, you'll be a tough nut to crack for those old- timers!"

"Well, I don't know what to tell you, Galek. Certainly, the channel's position is clearly biased. For example, can you believe that at this point your channel hasn't even given a small interview or a moment of airtime to Kelia Zaver? But almost every quint, all the others appear, especially Ragner, always saying the same crap... I debated for a long time whether I wanted to enter a channel like that or not, but I considered it a personal challenge to enter and try to do things differently..."

"Sure" added the young huno. "Moreover, the technological infrastructure and global reach it has could be used intelligently and strategically to disseminate information and achieve many good things..."

"Yes... but wait a minute, there's something I don't understand. If that's the case and you're so against the line of the group, why don't you just take over and stay in charge? You would have the power to change things…"

"No… I wouldn't… if I haven't been able to change my own father, do you think I'll be able to change his beloved creation? It's impossible, and my father knows it… and even less after the merger in which we became 'The World Source of Information'… What we really are now is almost like 'agents of the Z-Sunian government'. I wouldn't even be in charge of the editorial line as you say. That part is managed overseas now… He wants me there only as a nominal and financial representative of the family's interests but not to make decisions about the ideological inclination of the group."

"Well, but there's a difference between what they intend for you to do and what you will actually do."

"It's not that easy… Besides, I just want to be a normal person… and my family sees me as the transgressor for that…" He paused with a sight of sadness on his eyes, but immediately added:

"and by the way, you're diverting the topic. You are the one who's going to get in there and give headaches to my father's coven of wizards… ha ha ha!"

"Well, I'll think about it and let you know, okay?"

"All right."

They continued together for a while longer and then said goodbye. There was a greater closeness between them, and the next thía Galek didn't wait for Nissa's decision. He went straight to the Hunuman Resources department of the channel.

"Good thía, Galera Rúbik."

"How are you, Galar Zoren Zic? What a surprise! What brings you here today?"

"Very well, thank you. Galera Rúbik, do you happen to have the application of an informatist named Nissa Berdat among the candidates?"

"Let me see… yes, here it is" she searched among a pile, separated it from the rest, and placed it at the edge of the desk. "It was with the others who will go to the interview."

"Have you reviewed it yet?" Galek asked, concerned that she might have already noticed Nissa's profile.

"Not her specifically, no" Galera Rúbik replied.

"Phew, that's a relief!" thought Galek, and then he said: "Well, so probably you don't know and that is exactly why I came to talk to you, Galera Rúbik. My father knows this informatist and her work she is apparently extremely brilliant, he wants her on our crew and ordered that this huna be hired directly without going through the interview process."

"Hmm, I'm quite surprised, Galar Zoren Zic, and forgive me, but our hiring policy clearly state that all applicants must go through the interview and selection process. This department I lead is very strict and efficient, you know?" Galek realized this was going to be harder than he thought.

He knew Nissa would be rejected due to her history and tendencies, so he came up with a risky idea. He took out his nokó and pretended to call… "Okay, Galera Rúbik, don't worry. Let me directly tell my father your position." Galera Rúbik, with a victorious smile, nodded her head.

*https://opensea.io/collection/another-world-the-book*

However, her expression changed upon hearing the conversation.

"Hello, Mom, yes. I need to talk to dad urgently. I know that he is delicate and shouldn't speak, but I'm at the channel doing an errand he assigned to me, and I have to inform him that, according to the director's opinion, it can't be done. Yes, Mom, I know how dad gets when contradicted and that the doctor said he couldn't have strong emotions, but it's out of my hands. Tell him he has to speak directly with..." he said, turning towards the repentant huna…" who was already making desperate signs for him to end the call.

*https://opensea.io/collection/another-world-the-book*

"Oh no, no, Mom, it seems it's already resolved, thank you, I love you too, a kiss to Dad."

"No, Galar Zoren Zic, please, it wasn't necessary" said Galera Rúbik with a nervous smile.

"People understand each other by talking; it's just that I wanted them to know that I stick to the rules."

"Do not worry, Galera Rúbik, I understand, it was just that, since a few conjunctions ago the new mobile controller was hired without an interview and the new young huna in international news for the early dahna broadcast as well, I thought this would be done without any issues, especially coming directly from dad." Galek said this knowing that hires at the channel were handled in a shady and capricious manner, not – by the rulebook – as Galera Rúbik wanted to make it seem.

"Well… uh, yes, those were special cases galar…"

"Oh, just like this one also seems to be, Galera Rúbik."

"Yes, definitely, no doubts galar."

"Alright, Galera Rúbik, thank you very much, and apologize for any inconvenience."

"No, not at all, please excuse the misunderstanding."

"Don't worry, you're just doing your job. Have a good thía." Galek left the office with a bead of sweat on his forehead, took a deep breath, and left, but not before taking Nissa's resume and leaving only the form with the basic information. He didn't want any evidence of his friend's combative past. Meanwhile, Galera Rúbik picked up the nokó:

"Hello, Ban-Dinhu? Yes, yes... Look, I was reviewing the files you sent me for the interview, but the only one that meets the requirements is Madame Berdat's. What's going on, Ban-Dinhu? Any problem? Because if you have something to say, you can come upstairs and talk to me about it, face to face..." and she hung up the call, feeling relieved to be able to unload her frustration on the unfortunate subordinate.

Early the next thía, Nissa's nokó rang:

"Yes, good thía, is this Major[19] Berdat?"

"Speaking."

"We're calling from TUUS World Network. You filled out an application with us, correct?"

"Yes, several quints ago."

"We apologize for the delay in our response, but congratulations! If you're still interested in our offer, you've been selected as our new anchor for the 'In Depth' segment. We'd like to welcome you to our team. We need you to be at our facilities just after the start of thía tomorrow, at the Hunuman Resources Department, Office of Nara Rúbik, to discuss salary and benefits."

"Galek!" Nissa thought, and then replied, "Thank you very much! Yes, of course, I'll be there. See you tomorrow!" she said, still surprised.

"Perfect, congratulations! It's a pleasure to say, 'Welcome aboard!'"

Nissa remained thoughtful for a few moments until her nokó took her out of her introspection when it rang again; this time it was Galek.

---

19   Academic title obtained after finishing a professional study.

"Galek, what did you do?"

"Why, what are you talking about?" he asked, feigning surprise.

"They just called me from 'your' channel to start working tomorrow."

"Really?... That is great!!! Congratulations…!!!" After a silence from Nissa, Galek laughed and said: "First of all, that's not 'my' channel, and secondly, if you come out, I'll tell you all about it, and you can scold me over breakfast. How does that sound?" Curious and a bit flustered, Nissa peered out the window through the blinds and saw Galek outside, speaking from his vehicle. A smile spread across her face, a mix of affection and annoyance melting into fondness. She felt somehow then that whatever Galek had done, it was from a place of care and connection.

*https://opensea.io/collection/another-world-the-book*

As Nissa stepped out to meet him, the morning air felt different—crisp and filled with new possibilities. Over breakfast, Galek revealed that he had submitted her portfolio because he believed how her talent and dedication could impact not only the channel but in their country reality and people life's. This revelation, shared over shared laughter and playful banter, brought them closer, blurring the lines between professional respect and personal admiration.

Their conversations flowed effortlessly, touching on dreams, aspirations, and the whimsical turns of fate. As they shared these moments, it became clear that their bond had roots reaching far deeper than either had anticipated.

From that thía forward, their relationship blossomed against the backdrop of shared adventures and mutual support. This romance, sparked by a serendipitous act of caring, that morning that Nissa decided contact Galek, unfolded with a depth and richness that neither could have predicted.

Indeed, a romantic relationship began between two beings whose destinies were much more intertwined than either of them could have imagined.

---

Masaru entered his daughter Etzuko's apartment, loaded with all his luggage. He set it down on the floor and was struck by a photo of himself as a young huno, holding his little daughter. In the background, a rocket launch pad. He clearly remembered the moment of the photo.

Little Etzuko, surprised by the huge cloud of gases produced by a rocket launch, asked her father why they were polluting the air. Her father hugged her and explained,

"Daughter, haha, it's not smoke, it's mostly ákuah vapor. It's not as polluting as it seems… and besides, this is the only way they have today to travel to the stars… but someday we will travel to space and beyond without pollution, effortlessly, and with the help of something very, very tiny…" he said indicating the smallness with his fingers "so tiny that you can't even see it…"

"And something so tiny can move that humongous rocket?… I am big already, and I can't do it!" was the innocent response of the girl to her father's idealistic scenario. Both laughed as the father picked her up when a wandering photographer arrived.

"A photo with the girl, galar?"

"Yes, please!" was the response to the photographer's offer, capturing a moment that Etzuko cherished to this thía as a memory of a happy childhood with her father.

*https://opensea.io/collection/another-world-the-book*

Masaru went upstairs to his room and began unpacking, reflecting on everything that had happened in such a short time. He still couldn't believe it... Sitting on the bed, he pondered, just a few thías ago, he was working in his laboratory, and now he was here, in Akuahgrandia, with an uncertain future ahead of him. Deep in thought, he asked himself, "What am I missing? What am I not seeing? Should I continue with this? What if it's a obsession and it is simply impossible?" Lost in these thoughts, he fell asleep. In his dream, Masaru was driving towards a beautiful palace on the horizon. Suddenly, he reached a fork in the road. Turning right would continue his journey on the same road, while the left led to a path where he couldn't continue with his vehicle. He would have to abandon it and proceed on foot. It was a less-traveled, intricate path through a dense forest with lush but strange plants. It seemed sensible to him to continue on the road, which he did, only to find himself at the same fork again after some time of driving in circles... and then he woke up. His daughter had returned. Masaru shared his strange dream with Etzuko and then recounted his long story of victories and defeats, and how he ended up in Akuahgrandia with nothing but the notes and files from his research. Etzuko listened attentively, trying to comfort him. He appeared quite depressed, unsure of what would become of him at this stage of his life and career, in a foreign country without even an apparent plan. After some thought, she said:

"Dad, I have an idea. I know some people in the government; maybe I can get some help. I'm sure someone with your talent, knowledge, and experience can be useful to many people... Let's do something. Gather your information and organize it. I'm going to make some calls and let's hope things work out. I think something good can come from this."

---

The following thía, Mae-uhkel's curiosity about his downstairs neighbor and her pertinent words lingered. Why those words, and why then? She mentioned the heart, and he thought of the Core of Fire - could there be a connection? And what about the lights - were they the BR or merely a vision? His troubling encounter with Izora came to mind, but this felt different. Compelled to understand more, Mae-uhkel decided to visit the enigmatic elderly huna. He went down stairs and standing in front of the apartment, as he raised his hand to knock, the door swung open unexpectedly, leaving him rapping the air.

"Hello Mae-uhkel, good morning! Mistaken visit again?"

"Hello Galera Leyhana, well, not this time. I was hoping we could have a chat if you're not too busy."

"There is not such a thing as "too busy to chat" at this age son, please, come right in. I was about to start my meal."

Observing the table set for two, Mae-uhkel remarked, "I'm so sorry galera Leyhana, if you're expecting someone else, surely, I could come another time..."

"No, there's no one else but you and me. Why do you ask? Oh, the extra place setting? I set it for you, thinking you might be hungry this early..."

Mae-uhkel's surprise was evident, realizing Leyhana had anticipated his visit. To ease the unexpectedness, she urged, "Please, take a seat."

A delicious fragrance of fresh baked goods surrounding the space was the frame for a vibrantly colored table, adorned with an array of fruits and expertly prepared dishes. As they began their meal, Leyhana inquired,

"So, Mae-uhkel, what brings you to the home of this old huna?"

"Well, Galera Leyhana, your words really resonated in my head. Why did you say that at that moment?" Leyhana continued eating slowly, paused, and replied,

"I believe that's a question you already have the answer to, Mae-uhkel. I said what I felt I had to say at the moment it needed to be said. However, I think you're here for something more. More fruit?"

"Yes, I mean no" Mae-uhkel responded thoughtfully. "No more fruit, thank you, but perhaps I am indeed here for something more…" he continued, still absorbed in thought. He then wondered if it had been a bad idea to come after all, as it seemed Galera Leyhana really had nothing to offer him and probably that comment was nothing more than a coincidence; he decided to remain silent as they ate. As they were about to finish, Leyhana broke the silence:

"How about some hot drink? Finish while I clear the table…"

"Oh, yes, thank you. Everything was delicious, but no, please…" he replied, standing up and gathering the dishes, resolved to avoid further conversation and leave "I'll wash the dishes, galera Leyhana. It's the least I can do after such a delicious meal."

"On his way to the kitchen, Mae-uhkel's attention was drawn to several images neatly arranged on what seemed to be a worktable. Ships like those in his dreams, some in photographs, others in what looked like ancient writings, hieroglyphs, and even petroglyphs. However, most of the photos were of peculiar monoliths made of a vibrant green, crystalline rocky material, almost like gems, with rare text inscriptions carved into the living rock. The collection also included groups of handwritten note sheets, other photos of caves, people, and villages, as well as drawings, and a map of Hunum. It reminded him of his own wall. It appeared that galera Leyhana was also researching something. As he stood in front of the unusual array, Leyhana approached him and said:

"These…" she said, pointing to the monoliths, "…are the Quam-Ru Tablets. Have you heard of them?"

*https://opensea.io/collection/another-world-the-book*

"No."

"The legend says that every planet in the universe has a set of these Tablets. They are carved from this mineral, resonating with its green color, the green of Truth. It's believed they contain all the wisdom and laws governing the entire universe. Wise beings are sent to each world to channel them, create them, and leave them as a guide for the growth of the beings inhabiting those worlds. These are from Hunum, like a Handbook of Life."

"Wow!" he exclaimed, surprised, observing the monoliths in detail, pondering the profound implications they could have for hununmanity. A complete paradigm shift for history, religion, science... Then a question arose, "Tell me, galera, why, if something like this really exists, I have never heard of them before?"

"Because they were left to a civilization lost in history. Our ancestors, over a vast number of cycles ago, contrary to today's official and academic history beliefs, reached high scientific development but were sadly detached from the soul, leading to self-destruction"

"And why haven't remains of this civilization been found?" he asked skeptical

"Despite ample evidence across the planet, science hesitates to acknowledge the existence of such ancient civilizations. The evidence, not fitting the official narrative of the Academy, is dismissed. Moreover, despite its abundance, it's still insufficient to piece together and understand what really happened. We believe, just before the extinction caused by the rulers of hunumanity at the time, most inhabitants, innocent of the horrors, were taken off the planet and relocated to other worlds to continue their evolution. Only the few perpetrators remained, eventually perishing due to their actions. The aboriginal peoples, survivors living in remote areas, developed over time and are recognized by science today as 'evolutionary links of the first hunumans... but it's a misperception, a lack of understanding of the planet's true past, as no trace of these events remained."

"Let me see if I got this right." He said trying to find a sense on everything the elder was telling him "You're saying that there was an ancient civilization here on Hunum, older than recognize by science, that reached a high level of development but also caused its destruction... and when mass extinction was imminent, most of them, innocent in the events, were... removed? But by whom?"

"We don't know for sure yet, but these ships seem having something to do with it — she said, picking up several images. — They've been sighted and photographed by thousands around Hunum, and there are many historical accounts from ancient civilizations, even in the sacred books of various religions, suggesting their involvement, not just in that event, but many throughout hunumanity's history. One possibility is they belong to outer Hunum civilizations...

This last comment rise Mae-uhkel's attention due to his recurring dreams and interest grew as he listened to Leyhana's stories. However, he inquired yet skeptical:

"But doesn't this suggest the existence of intelligent life beyond the Thía system? We know it's uninhabited, except for us on Hunum, right? Unless, of course, these beings are far more advanced than we are and are coming from way far, far away?"

"Good questions and the answers to those and others are what I've been researching. What we do know is that the tablets are written in a language unknown to us. These symbols" she said, pointing to the engravings on the crystal green rocks,

"And what do they say?"

"We don't know yet... only small segments of the text have been revealed here and there by external sources discussing the content of the tablets."

"And why, with all our advances, haven't we deciphered it?" He asked not very convinced with all that mysterious story.

"The Light of Real Knowledge does not come from the mind and isn't for everyone. Those who've lived in darkness all their lives, upon seeing such a light, might be blinded forever. The legend also says that the teachings of the Quam- Ru Tablets must be deserved, earned, and can only be unveiled and understood under one sole Light" she said, placing her hand on his shoulder, then paused before adding, "The Light of the Heart... That light we all possess and which… you are able to see…"

Mae-uhkel was paralyzed, pale, and bewildered. How did Leyhana know about his visions? But now, it all started to make sense regarding her. Agitated, he removed her hand from his shoulder, stepped back, and exclaimed, "Who are you, and what do you know about me?"

"I am Leyhana, and I know you are Mae-uhkel, the son of Galera Granahoi, from upstairs…"

" Stop with that... — He interrupted her — Do not play any more games with me! How do you know about my visions? Have you told anyone else?"

"Calm down, my son, no, I haven't spoken of this to anyone. Please, calm down..." she requested gently and continued "You should know what's happening to you is not an illness or a curse. It's a gift, a precious gift... you have the ability to perceive beyond your physical senses... and your father had it too, only that he never came to recognize it." Mae-uhkel fell to his knees, bursting into tears. Leyhana stay back and after a moment, embraced him, comforting a soul finally freed from the heavy weight of so many cycles of suffering. He cried long and after a silence of relieving, he managed to speak through sobs.

"Since I was little... many, including the Sha Quara of the oratory, called me strange, said I should seek help... that it wasn't Gaemo's stuff..."

*https://opensea.io/collection/another-world-the-book*

"Gaemo is EVERYTHING, Mae-uhkel, and EVERYTHING happens for a reason, for a purpose.

We just have to discover and fulfill it — she said, comforting him, helping him regain calmness.

Seeing him more at ease, she added "All is well, go home, my son. Rest, you need it. There will be time for us to talk later." Mae-uhkel nodded and silently walked with her to the door, leaving dejected but deep down feeling light and profoundly grateful, thinking that he would finally have answers and, most importantly, he wasn't crazy, nor was his father.

# CHAPTER III

## UNVEILING

That danha, Mae-uhkel went to bed pondering about his father... he had always resented him for leaving them, but now he understood his pain a bit more. His visions were real, but he was unable to convince anyone, not even himself, that they were, let alone manage them. He was branded as mad, and thus began his hell. Mae-uhkel felt compassion. As he meditated on this, he fell into a deep sleep. In his dream, he was walking in a park and soon realized he was not alone. It was his father! Seeing him, he embraced him, and they continued walking in silence.

*https://opensea.io/collection/another-world-the-book*

Tears welled up in his eyes as he expressed:

"I'm sorry, but I needed you so much..."

"I know, son, and I'm the one who owes an apology, to you and your mother... I suffered like never before in life because of my decisions, but the worst of all was taking my own life, as it only perpetuated my suffering. I woke up in a dark and gloomy world, a quagmire of anguish and desolation, and I stayed there for what felt like an eternity. Surrounded by beings as tormented, if not more, than I was. They cursed Gaemo for their condition. Not knowing if I was alive or dead, I tried to end my life again and that's when I discovered I no longer belonged to the world of the living. The visions and terrifying beings that I occasionally saw in life, now in that place, haunted me constantly. I wandered and lost myself, and when I had nothing left to cling to, I cried out to Gaemo for help.

*https://opensea.io/collection/another-world-the-book*

I was only able to leave that place when I understood and learned. I learned that ending my physical life did not solve my problems; it only made them worse... I also learned that life is meant to be lived, not fixed and to use our abilities to love it and others. Situations, sweet or bitter, everything is a lesson. We go through what we need to grow... Now I am well, and you will be too... I want to try again..." They walked a few steps in silence, and finally, he said while kissing his forehead, "I love you and am proud and grateful to life for letting me be near you and have been your father... you are greater than you can imagine..." fading away as he spoke.

Mae-uhkel opened his eyes, still filled with tears, and sighed with a smile.

"I love you too, dad" he said, then noted the details of his dream and continued sleeping, from that moment on, more deeply than he had in cycles.

Awakening at dawn, he leapt from his bed and rushed to Leyhana's house. Checking the krono, he realized it might be too early to knock on his friend's door. Hesitating, wondering if it was too soon to disturb her, he approached the entrance of the apartment, looking for any sign she might be awake. At that moment, Leyhana opened the door.

"Good morning, Mae-uhkel! Come in, let's sit down. Something tells me this will be a long conversation, and..." Mae-uhkel interrupted her with a hug, expressing his gratitude for her words and empathy the thía before. Leyhana smiled, moved, hugging him back. The young huno eagerly started to recount his dream about his father, but Leyhana interjected:

" Son, son, wait, before we start talking, I need to tell you something... It's important." Mae-uhkel paused in his narrative to listen to what seemed like an important disclosure from the serious look on his friend's face.

"You must promise me not to believe anything I tell you from this point on."

Mae-uhkel's mood shifted from joy to confusion at her strange request, as he was expecting answers to many questions he had. Leyhana continued:

"I say this because anything I might tell you will be the product of my own search, learning, and growth process and will provide my perspective on things. You can use it as a guide, but it's your duty, as it is for all beings in the universe, to seek your own Truth, inside yourself, in your heart, as I told you the first time you came to my door. You must polish your own lens, view The Truth through it. Any truth you think you hear from another person, never fully believe it; verify it by yourself, make it your own, and move from belief to certainty. Otherwise, you'll fall into what all religions and science of Hunum have, into the darkness and sterility of dogma. Promise me that!"

Mae-uhkel nodded.

"Very well, then, what were you saying about a dream?"

"Yes, I dreamed about my father yesterday" he paused slightly "but it felt very real, like some dreams I often have. They feel very real, you know?"

"I believe it, as sometimes they might be. Also, I think dreams sometimes contain teachings in the form of symbols, sometimes experiences, sometimes visions of the past, and even premonitions..."

"So, are you saying it could have been real?" Mae-uhkel looked at her, "that I actually spoke to him?"

"I don't know, but why not? At the end, who defines real? what is real?... but tell me more."

"He told me.." Mae-uhkel paused "wait! I wrote it here in my notebook..." The young huno opened his notebook and searched through his notes "that he spent a long time in a horrible place,

I didn't quite understand, that he regretted committing suicide and that life was to be lived and our abilities used to help others. He apologized to me and my mom... He also told me that he is now well and that he was proud of who I was..."

"Hmm, interesting... And what didn't you understand?"

"Well, he said he spent an immeasurable amount of time in a dark and gloomy place from which he could only escape when he understood and learned..."

"Oh, well, that could be because, as I understand, when we die, we create around us a world according to our mental and emotional state, along with others in similar states; usually, those who take their lives are tormented, and that is what their realities reflect in the other side. Maybe later we can talk about that but... How do you feel after that experience?"

"Oh, very relieved, – he said, then added, – I was able to feel compassion and was happy to see him and also have the opportunity to apologize to him as well for so many years of resentment..."

" That exactly is what makes it real to you. Those feelings of forgiveness, compassion and understanding set you free and that is what defines your reality. I'm glad to hear that. Well, but let's start then; the first thing is to understand the extent of your abilities, tell me a bit about them."

"Yes…" The boy went back to the old notes in his notebook and showed her, on his nokó, photos of his wall, explaining what they were about. During several hours of lengthy conversation, Mae-uhkel spoke about the classification he had made and how and when he had his visions. He also explained that he had no control over them nor knew what triggered them.

After the long explanation, Leyhana was silent, and Mae-uhkel inquired:

"So, what do you think, galera Leyhana? Please don't stay silent" he added, a hint of concern in his voice.

Breaking the tension, Leyhana finally spoke

"It is simply fascinating, Mae-uhkel, I've never known anyone with such a spectrum… look what I mean" Leyhana stood and retrieved writing instruments. As she began to draw and explain, she said, "Look, what we all know as 'reality' is not singular; it's actually a fusion of various realities. It's made up of layers upon layers, permeable among themselves, meaning they are in contact with each other; these layers are the different realities or dimensions. We, hunumans, live in the third layer or dimension. We are able to understand and perceive lower dimensions but higher dimensions are imperceptible to most. The beings and energies you observe: Gaemas, Tumsas, Bham-yis, as you've named them, belong to, operate in more subtle dimensions… Come, follow me." They headed to the work table. "I've known and studied people around Hunum with similar gifts to yours" she said, reaching for some of the graphics.

"Each one with gifts similar to yours… This one, for example, perceived the Light of the heart in people. This one here, a clairaudient, capable of hearing the thoughts of others, living physical beings and also some others invisible to her. These twins can communicate with each other telepathically and claimed to have contact with luminous beings.

*https://opensea.io/collection/another-world-the-book*

This one: remote vision, this the power of healing… and many more, all capable of seeing or hearing some of the things you manage. But I had never met anyone with such a broad spectrum of perception. No doubt it's something you've been working on and developing for a long time" she said thoughtfully.

"Not really, Galera Leyhana, I never heal anybody and as I told you, I've had visions since I was a child, and it's spontaneous."

"No Mae-uhkel, I mean from lives before this one." Mae-uhkel's look of confusion showed Leyhana she needed to explain.

"Look Mae-uhkel, 'death' as we, common hunuman beings, know it, is an illusion. What people call dying is just a change of garments. The breaths of life coming from Gaemo are eternal. As beings growing from and towards Gaemo, we must learn from all experiences and actions against life we commit. In fact, as you've inferred, the 'common' invisible beings are people who went through this 'dying' process and haven't accepted or understood it. They refuse to continue their evolutionary path and remain tied to this world out of fear of what comes next, ignorance, or stubbornness." Mae-uhkel recalled the common invisibles he saw at Izora's office. "Once the being leaves its garment and accepts it, it passes to the mental-emotional world I mentioned, and there, through a process of learning and reflection on the assimilated and ignored, the actions and omissions in the life that just ended, plans its next life. And thus, the being 'reincarnates' over and over, learning from its different experiences, leading to growth. If any act is committed that hurts or harms the Law of Love, it will return and live experiences that help understand and assimilate the fact that what you do to others, you do to yourself. That's why we are born again and again, growing more and more, thanks to the learning we have thía after thía."

"And what happened to my father then?"

"I don't know, but I can think that he spent a long time in that tormented state and now will be in the process of reflection and planning his next incarnation. In it, he will surely face similar situations to those he experienced before and that led him to do what he did, as an opportunity to practice what he learned and grow…"

"Now I understand what he meant when he said, 'I want to try again'."

"Oh, did he say that? Interesting, because inside, we all have the innate desire in our hearts to grow, to be Love and that's why during this journey of lives that we are developing, we accumulate virtues, abilities, and also defects, mistakes, growing, moving up 'layers' in the onion, and eventually becoming 'Gaemas' and even beyond. I was telling you all this to explain that such a developed gift, like the one you have, is undoubtedly the product of many lives of work and development. You said you can't heal. Healing requires the use of all those forces consciously, so once you get control over your capabilities, you'll be able to do amazing things that surely you were able to do in your past lives. You've probably gained a lot of habits and discipline that nowadays are such a part of yourself that you don't even notice them. Look, let me show something, I noticed you weren't bothered by something that might be curious and even uncomfortable for most. I had nothing of what is considered the regular diet for most, I only offered you vegetable foods and fruits yesterday for breakfast, why is that?"

"Well, actually I liked it because I only eat plants… for health and ethical reasons, I love animals, and the idea of exploiting them or worse, killing them to eat doesn't appeal to me at all and I don't think it's necessary… I've seen a lot of information about its benefits too, and I usually take great care of what I put into my body, so I liked the idea and embraced it."

"Could you say that you 'felt' it suited you?"

"I think so, yes."

"You see, that's something you already know, but don't realize you know it..." Leyhana explained, seeing Mae-uhkel's confused expression." It's known that to fully develop your psychic abilities, which is what you do, is better to keep your physical body clean; this is knowledge that you surely have internally, in your subconscious, but you don't remember. Participation in the killing process to consume animal carcasses intoxicates, hinders interdimensional connection, and robs you of your vital energy, just like constant hatred, drugs, and all habits that create dependency.

"The Bham-yis! I've seen them do that!"

"Exactly! See? Those Bham-yis, as you call them, are individual energy creations. They are called Entities in other cultures. People think they are victims of their 'vices,' as they call them. They think it's a 'disease' that needs to be cured. What they don't know is that they are real energy forms with their own life, created by themselves, attached to them by energy threads, feeding off them, like umbilical cords connecting them to their 'parents.' They are created from repeated behavior where we focus our attention and energy. This accumulates to form an entity that takes on a life of its own and then demands that energy to continue living. A habit, a Bham-yi is created. The more we feed it with repeated attention, energy," and action, the stronger it becomes and the more forcefully it will later demand from us. These are the so-called 'withdrawal crises.' If people knew they are not 'slaves' to their vices but their masters, their creators, and just as they created them, they can also dissolve them, then they could easily free themselves from them. And look, you wrote something similar on your wall: 'They seem to represent the vices and harmful habits of people through which they absorb their energy, as if feeding on it'; all this you know internally, surely from having learned and practiced it in other lives, now it's part of you and manifests in that way.

"Ok, but then, I should be able to control it!"

"Well, not necessarily, Mae-uhkel, and here's why. We are dual beings, like these two fingers,

"she said, showing him her index and middle fingers together" Some scholars of these subjects have called this duality hunuman Self and Master Self, implying it's beyond the hunuman or simply Soul. The Master Self is Eternal in time, does not die and cumulates all of our ancient wisdom. When we come to this third dimension, we need a vehicle to navigate this reality, and it's new and different in each incarnation. This is the hunuman Self, or 'the Impostor,' because of its physical condition, it fills up with fears and beliefs and it grows on them, however pretends to be who we are, each one of us... It makes us believe that we are it, and we identify with it, to the point of making it the master of our life. Little do we know that without those fears and beliefs we'd become the Master Self. Most people ignore all this and live their whole lives under the command of the Impostor. Slaves believing themselves to be free. This hunuman Self, being 'new,' must 'remember' who the being hosting it is, relearn, or rather 'reteach' itself what it's capable of, become conscious, awake. In short, reconnect with its Eternal Self or Master Self."

"And how?"

"Ah, that's the question I was expecting. It's here that the light of the heart comes into play. This is the contact point through which we reconnect with our Master Self and thus access Gaemo. The more you journey in the Light and strengthen your connection consciously, the brighter the light shines, and vice versa. The more decisions against Love we make when acting out of fear or damaging beliefs, the more our light fades, and the connection closes. You isolate yourself from your Source, and you dry up, lifeless…"

"Oh yes, I've noticed that with the Invisible Commoners… some of them that look very tormented seem to darken."

"Yes, and if they continue down that path, the tormented may end up as tormentors…"

"Tumsas!!! Wow, but wait a moment," he paused, conflicted. "So, if this is the origin of Tumsas they are also children of Gaemo?"

"Loving and compassionate observation. Indeed, as the journey is eternal, there's always free will to act a certain way and then, if deemed necessary, to rectify at any moment. Every being has the ability and opportunity to choose who to serve, their Master or the Impostor, ALWAYS our decision. With a simple act of acknowledgment and rectification, a Tumsa can resume its path back to the Light. In fact, all of us, Gaemo's children, can accelerate our journey, developing and expanding our connection, becoming more conscious, understanding our emotions thus being more in control of ourselves, thoughts and ideas, even our senses... the physical and non-physical ones, to put them at the service of the hunuman needs which are the voice of the Light in everyone..."

"Really? And how is that achieved?"

"Well, they are many ways and the main idea of all of them is to quiet the mind, the voice of the Impostor. I can show one simple way right now. Come on, sit here, this is one the ancients used to seek that reconnection. This, if practiced daily, helps awaken our sensitivity... but I suppose it will be a bit easier for you since it's so close to the surface for you." Once Mae-uhkel sat down, Leyhana play a strange instrument that emitted a monotonous but sweet and deep sound. She then said "It's a simple but powerful exercise. The sound helps you focus on something taking the attention away from the mind. Now relax, focus on the sound, immerse yourself in it and breathe deeply, several times, then gradually let your body breathe normally and allow your mind to rest and quieten."

"I know how to do that, I practice Bayheme."

"Oh, very good, then breathe as in Bayheme; try to feel your heart beating and now focus your attention there, on the breathing and the heartbeat. Let go of any though, any issue, worries... just observe the sensations in your body as you breathe, be aware of your body breathing here and now, the past is gone, the future is not here yet. You just have here and now. Inhaling, exhaling, don't try to control your breathing or your thoughts, just observe them, contemplate it, feel the flow of air through your nose, flowing into your body; with each breath you begin to realize that your mind wanders... bring it back to the breath, each time, bring it back.

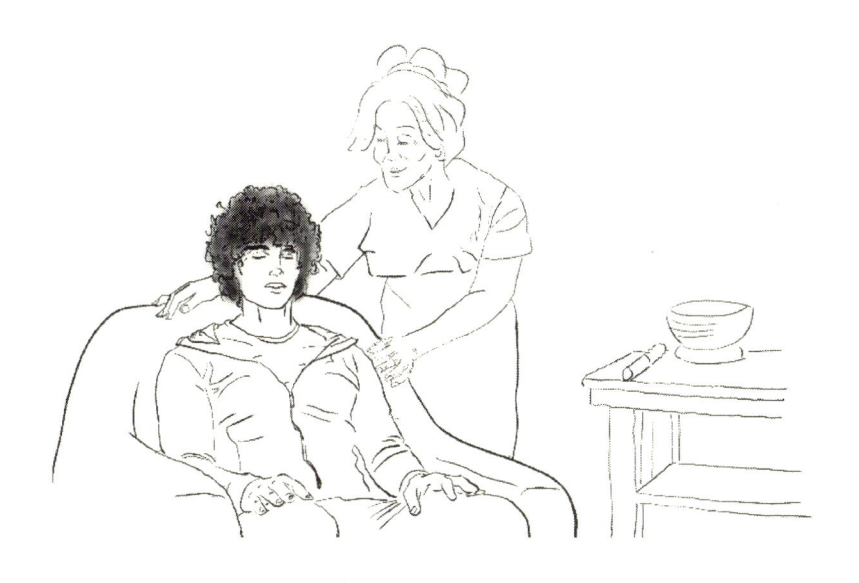

*https://opensea.io/collection/another-world-the-book*

This way, your attention focuses, and your mind doesn't wander even in an alert state. It will help you develop your abilities while staying focused. Now you go deeper and deeper, feel one with the breath and comfortably rest in it. Feel yourself as one with everything…"

After several moments following Leyhana's guidance, Mae-uhkel experienced a strange but pleasant sensation throughout his body, a tingling; until he lost awareness of himself, his body, time and space, and saw himself floating in the void, surrounded by intense white light, but no, not surrounded, he was merged with it, he was Light, he was Everything… He didn't know how long he was in that state, but upon coming out of that trance, he got up from the chair and went straight to Leyhana's worktable, looked at the photos, then spoke as if possessed by a strange force:

*"The ALL is MIND, is CONSCIOUSNESS; the universe is mental. EVERYTHING first occurs in the Mind. This is the power of powers, the father of every miraculous work in the whole world. It's true, certain, and beyond all doubt, that what is above comes from what is below, and what is below comes from what is above. All dimensions are similar. Thus, the small world is created according to the prototype of the great world. From this and*

*in this way, wonderful things are made... Nothing is still; everything moves; EVERYTHING vibrates. Vibration conquers all subtle things and penetrates all vast things; it separates earth from fire and the subtle from the vast, gently and with great prudence... As all things proceed from the One by meditation on the one, so they are also born from Him. EVERYTHING is apparently dual, but in reality, it is ONE, everything seems to have two poles; everything, its pair of opposites: but the like and the antagonistic are the same; opposites are identical in nature, but different in degree; extremes meet; all truths are half-truths, all paradoxes can be reconciled. The subtle rises from the earth to the sky and descends again from the sky to the earth, and thus acquires the power of the higher and lower things. In this way, it acquires the glory of the whole world, and all darkness flees from him. Everything flows and ebbs; everything has its periods of advance and retreat; everything ascends and descends; everything moves like a pendulum; rhythm is compensation. Every cause has its effect; every effect has its cause... Its Father is Thia, and its Mother Dahna. Gender exists everywhere; everything has its masculine and feminine principle; gender manifests on all planes of existence. EVERYTHING HAPPENS ACCORDING TO THESE LAWS, NO ONE AND NOTHING ESCAPES THEM."*

After this revelation, he opened his eyes and found himself back in the chair where it all began. They looked into each other's eyes and simultaneously exclaimed "The Tablets!" Excited, Mae-uhkel explained "I saw everything so clearly in my head, the meaning of the symbols clearly in my mind, I think there are seven laws…"

"Wait!" Leyhana interrupted him, "first, how do you feel?" she inquired, examining him from head to toe.

"Very well, Galera Leyhana" he replied, but as he got up from the chair, his legs faltered. "Oh, I'm dizzy, but I'm fine, it must be because I got up too quickly… Don't worry, what's important now is what we have. The Seven Laws, let's see, the first one is Everything is Mind; that's why you said that when people die, they create their worlds according to their mental-emotional state, right?"

"Yes, it seems so" Leyhana said, still closely observing Mae-uhkel's condition.

"Ok, then the second one talks about 'The Onion'," he said while pacing back and forth, threading his thoughts together. "I think, because it says dimensions are similar… That's why the garden where I spoke with my dad was so real, just like a hunuman garden. So, combining this second law with the first, if in the dimension where we go after death, we create our reality with the mind and the dimensions are similar, then in this reality, we should also be capable of doing it."

"You're right, Mae-uhkel, brilliant deduction!"

"Then the third, the third?... Help me, Galera Leyhana, please."

"Yes, yes. Here I noted what you said: Nothing is still; everything moves; EVERYTHING vibrates."

"Exactly! The Filament Theory, you know? I study Applied Psychophysics, and it's a relatively new theory that also asserts that, at the elemental level, everything, animate or inanimate, is like strings, nano filaments vibrating at different frequencies... We are tuning, see? At nano level, we are like microscopic radios that by tuning to a certain frequency, we join it, we become it; EVERYTHING VIBRATES, fascinating. Please continue, what about the fourth?"

"From that one, I have some notes from before your reading... it talks about the unity of Gaemo. Opposites don't really exist. Darkness is Light to a lesser degree, cold is heat to a lesser degree, hate is Love to a lesser degree; division doesn't really exist, it's a hunuman illusion, because Everything is One."

"I understand, so Gaemas, Tumsas, Commons, we're all the same, beings on the way back to the One, please, we must review them one by one later!; let's see, the next one is..." he said, checking Leyhana's notes, "The subtle rises from the earth to the sky... Hmm, hmm. Everything ascends and descends; everything moves like a pendulum; rhythm is compensation. This one isn't clear to me either..."

"I think it refers to the fact that Everything has a rhythm: sometimes we are up, we feel well, full, and happy, and sometimes we are down, then sadness, fear, anxiety, depression, and sometimes even pessimism invade us. If we manage to feel the rhythm of life, then we can better ride the wave when it's in its valley so that it affects us as little as possible and thus maintain a constant state of optimism, certainty, and fullness."

"I understand," Mae-uhkel nodded, "and we will be able to feel it when we reconnect through the heart, as you mentioned."

"That's right" the elder replied.

"Great! The next one I think is clear, Cause and Effect: everything has a cause that causes it, every action has a reaction, also in psychophysics we study something similar."

"Yes, it also implies that there really is no such thing as chance. Everything happens for a reason and for a purpose, as I mentioned earlier."

"Of course, I can see now that if this knowledge is so ancient, our science today is only rediscovering everything."

"Yes, my child, that's right," she said, smiling, then continued. "Of the last one, I also had some information. It implies that everything contains a masculine and feminine principle. To create anything, both forces, both energies in perfect harmony are needed."

"Wow, you're right; the content is incredible, Galera Leyhana, and the fact that we were able to decipher it is very important. Now we should develop the content; when I got up and read them, I realized…"

Leyhana interrupted him. "Mae-uhkel, wait a moment, you never got up from the chair."

"What? No, I did get up and went to the table, I saw the photos of the tablets, and this time I understood their content perfectly…" –

"No," she interrupted again, "you just started talking while sitting. It must have been an out-of-body experience. Your physical body was in the chair, and your more subtle body was the one that read; that's why you're dizzy; it's a process that demands a lot of energy, that's why I was attentive to how you felt. Well, then, that's enough for now…"

"But no, I'm fine," Mae-uhkel insisted. "Well, a little weak, but nothing more; please, we must work more on the tablets," he pleaded, sensing the start of something incredible…

"Yes, but we can continue later. We both need to rest, I'm also a bit drained."

"Ok…you're right, but I'll come back very early tomorrow so we can continue."

"Tomorrow will be another thía," Leyhana said, taking his shoulder and leading him to the door. Mae-uhkel left, still eager to continue, but understanding his friend's fatigue, and deeply grateful for the infinite knowledge she had shared in just a few hours of conversation with her. It was a magical evening of discoveries and awakenings.

# CHAPTER IV,

## – A DREAM TO AWAKEN, –

That evening, Mae-uhkel went to bed with his head full of ideas and questions about what he had just experienced at Leyhana's house. Eager for answers, he tried the exercise he had learned again, but fatigue overcame him, and he fell asleep. In his dream, he found himself in a vast hall, bathed in a soft, luminous pale magenta. Suddenly, he heard a voice in his head: "My Gheldar! Welcome, we've been expecting you."

"I've heard that before", Mae-uhkel thought, searching in all directions for the source of the voice in his head. The appearance of a beautiful Gaema beside him took him by surprise; the being was very tall, with reddish hair and skin like autumnal gold, features of perfect symmetry, and 'the symbol' emblazoned on its chest. Mae-uhkel felt profoundly loved.

"Where am I? What is this place?" he wondered. "We are in the Archive of Ages", the radiant being replied. It could hear his thoughts! "And who are you?" Mae-uhkel asked. "For now, consider me your guide in this experience."

"Why are we here?"

"Because your heart is full of questions, and you are ready to know a story that will give you answers."

"But I'm dreaming…"

"I would say you are awakening… One who looks outward dreams;

one who looks inward awakens. You have begun to look within, and it's this introspective search that has brought you here. Dreams are often experiences that contain teachings for the being and are more real than 'daily reality'." Mae-uhkel remembered Leyhana's words from hours earlier. "Come, follow me," the guide said, extending a hand.

*https://opensea.io/collection/another-world-the-book*

Mae-uhkel took the being's hand, and together they walked through the place:

"Here, everything that has happened, is happening, and will happen in the Universe is recorded. As you know from your studies, space and time are a continuum; there is no past, present, or future, only here and now. Everything you see is thanks to the light reflected by things. Energy is never destroyed, only transformed, meaning all light rays that have existed and exist are recorded in this Great Archive."

The place had many entrances, all covered with fluid curtains of multiple, changing colors. They moved toward one of them, and as they did, the fluid bubbled and then disappeared, revealing a majestic Gaema behind it, who looked at them with a loving but firm gaze, seemingly guarding the door; a nod of approval allowed them entry into a space where countless luminous spheres the size of a hand floated in a rhythmic and gentle sway. The guide took one of them and brought it closer.

*https://opensea.io/collection/another-world-the-book*

As Mae-uhkel touched it, he felt absorbed, entering another reality where he moved at the speed of thought through what he identified as the Thía solar system, leading him to Hunum's neighboring planet, Zax. There, the landscape was that of his recurring dream. Surprised, he exclaimed:

"This is impossible... this world cannot be Zax... Hunum is the only inhabited planet in the Thía solar system, there's no life on Zax, let alone intelligent life, there's nothing, it's a desert! Space probes have photographed almost the entire planet..."

"Because they only know how to see with physical eyes, but there are worlds within worlds, Mae- uhkel. Dimensions invisible to most, that's why they also can't see what you see.

"...All dimensions are similar", he said, remembering the Second Law. Several ships crisscrossed the skies in multiple directions. He could better perceive details of each of the beings he had seen before.

Their diverse, simple, and colorful attire matched their illuminated faces, joyful, youthful, devoid of suffering, and full of wisdom. The 'city' seemed to be the entire planet. They utilized all available space and didn't congregate in one place. There were no skyscrapers or tall buildings. The structures were a harmonious part of the natural pattern, without straight lines. Instead, beautiful curves that made them blend with the morphology and diversity of the lush vegetation. He finally arrived at a kind of complex of buildings divided by what seemed like work patios. Diverse beings performing equally diverse activities. At the entrance, symbols similar to those of the Quam-Rú tablets were engraved, but now Mae-uhkel could read them perfectly: 'Center for Enlightenment and Development of Knowledge of the One – The Light of the Heart Reveals The Truth'. He entered a kind of amphitheater, where he saw a rather tall figure, with dark hair and greenish complexion, radiating great wisdom in his gaze, speaking to a group of other similar beings but of shorter stature, who had in front of them holographic images transmitted by a very small cubic device.

"Love, Wisdom, and Will to all, young ones!" said the tall figure with a strong yet clear voice, emanating from his chest, at the level of the heart, three spheres of energy in Magenta, Yellow, and Blue colors. Immediately, a wave of similar but more intense energy moved from each member of the audience to the speaker, reciprocating his morning blessing.

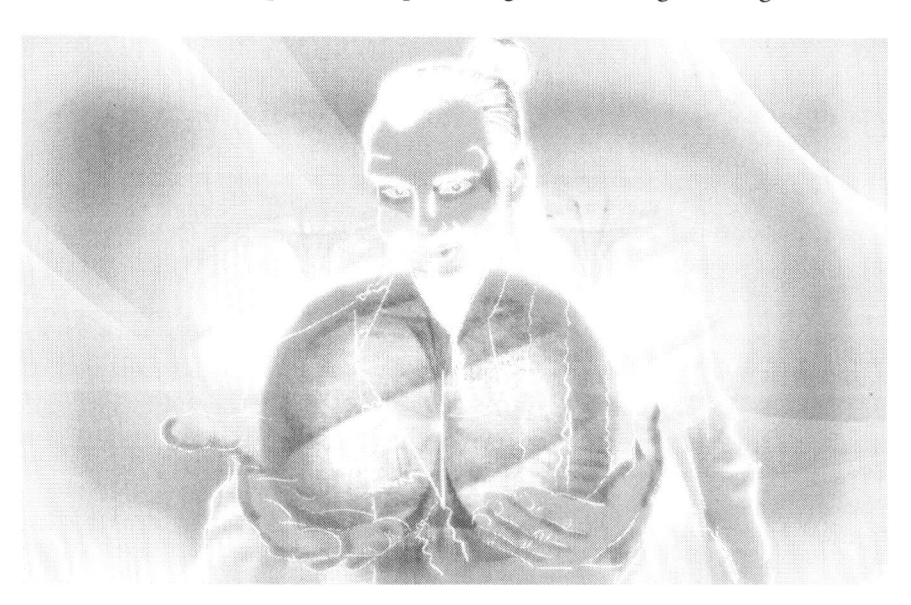

*https://opensea.io/collection/another-world-the-book*

The guide, sensing Mae-uhkel's question, explained: "What you just witnessed is a common greeting in these worlds. Unlike the automatic convention in Hunum, here, it's done with the phrase 'Love, Wisdom, and Will.' It's a true gift of energization of the three primary attributes of the One shared regularly among each other. You see, Mae-uhkel, Divinity possesses seven main virtues, and everything in the universe is formed by a combination of these. They also reside in every being's heart and are used daily in our actions. As an individual gains more self-mastery, they perfect the ability to manipulate these virtues at will. Each virtue vibrates at its own frequency, thus correlating with one of the seven prismatic colors. Love, Wisdom, and Will are represented by Magenta, Gold, and Blue, respectively, forming the basic and original three. Derived from them are Truth and Healing in green" Mae-uhkel remembered Leyhana... 'Carved in that mineral by the vibration of its color, green of Truth.' "Service, Giving, and Receiving in thíaset[20] and Transmutation and Purification in Violet, which transform negative energies and thoughts into positive ones also used to purify oneself and environment, removing discordant energies that hinder progress. The union of these six gives rise to the seventh, the white of Consecration and Elevation. That is the light you can see... The level of 'consecration' or achievement of a being in its evolutionary journey back to the Love of the One.

"Amazing! But you said, 'every being that exists.' Does that mean I can do it too?"

"Of course, Mae-uhkel, not just you, all your siblings in Hunum could if they knew of its existence. By focusing and expanding the light of the heart, just imagine emanating the desired virtue in its corresponding color, surrounding the condition or person in that energy. This will 'tune' you to its vibrational frequency, allowing you to emanate it from your heart."

"Right... everything vibrates. And it's that simple?"

"Yes, simple but very powerful. Try it and see for yourself. But now, let's observe the beginning of today's gathering." The guide said pointing back to the scene.

"Young ones" continued the wise being "as you know, being in the final stage at the Center of Illumination, the Eternal Law gives you the opportunity to serve with other brethren on a Third-Dimension planet in need, providing immense service to its inhabitants and the One, and, of course, offering you great and rapid advancements in your evolutionary path.

---

20 Color orange

The mission I will discuss today will be on our closest younger sibling, Hunum; it's planned for two of our cycles, equivalent to a complete incarnation, about a hundred hunuman cycles. Its success and subsequent return, as you all know, depend on your performance during each of your lives in the mission. Those interested, please let us know at the end of today's Forum in your qelca."

At that moment, Mae-uhkel's attention was drawn to a conversation between two attendees nearby:

"It would be an interesting experience, don't you think, Almog? And if it could bring us faster growth, it's worth the effort."

"It won't be easy, Fahel" replied Almog "It's something to consider carefully. I feel as if I'm not yet ready to face the harshness of the Third Dimension again. It's still hard for me to understand how most don't realize they're musicians in the same concert. That their actions, positive or negative, affect themselves and their siblings. It seems they don't even know they are siblings! Besides Fahel, while it's true that undertaking such a task means a significant evolutionary leap, one must consider the implications and risks..."

"Come on, it's just two cycles, almost like a tourism trip, although there it's 'a whole lifetime,' ha, ha, ha... No, but seriously, I want to advance, grow, become greater, and I'm willing to assume and face everything" were Fahel's last words to his friend before activating his qelca decisively and without hesitation. Suddenly, they left the 'scene' and were back in the Main Archive; Mae-uhkel was pensive, and after a brief silence, he affirmed: "If all this is real…" The beautiful being smiled, pleased with what Mae-uhkel was about to say "…then, is Leyhana's story true, and the beings she speaks of, are you… EXTRAHUNUMANS?"

"We've been called a thousand names throughout your history: extrahunumans, gods, tutelary geniuses, nature spirits, angels, 'Gaemas.' But the reality is that we are all just siblings, inhabitants of the concert of worlds in the universe. It falls to the greater ones to take care of our smaller siblings… like Hunum. We have been doing it since the first hunumans set foot on the planet and even before that, as was done with us in the past. Just as you will do in the future with those who follow. Today, you are already doing it; it's your responsibility to care for animals, plants, and the planet. It's an eternal cycle of Love… of giving.

"So those images of extrahunumans invading Hunum or abducting hunumans…"

"Are ideas meant to be implanted in the minds of the masses for various purposes; some as innocent as entertainment, others as calculated and harmful as instilling fear in their hearts and distancing them further from us. Fear is control."

"Oh, and now that I remember… I was thinking about what happened to the hunumans who were taken ten thousand cycles ago and those who were left behind?"

"Back then, the destruction was limited to a region of Hunum, as was the extraction of inhabitants. The first group continued their evolution on other worlds, according to their level, and we didn't 'leave' the others. Exercising their free will, they acted according to their excessive ambitions and only reaped the consequences of their actions…"

"Cause and Effect" Mae-uhkel said thoughtfully

"Believing in their dominion, they thought themselves omnipotent and immune to the harm they would inflict on others. They built shelters to hide in while carrying out their extermination. But their calculations did not account for the Eternal Law governing the universe, and by the time they realized their error, it was too late. They destroyed the entire region of the planet they inhabited and were trapped in it, living in the conditions they themselves created. In Third Dimension worlds, we learn to discern, but the process is arduous and sometimes very painful. "Now I understand what Alnog meant by 'implications and risks.'"

"His name is Almog, and yes, missions on Third Dimension planets are not simple, as you see. They require the cultivation of all the qualities of the One in order to avoid, as much as possible, any mistakes, so frequent and easy in those evolutionary links, which could lead them to remain tied to the planet's reincarnation wheel until they understand and overcome their fault. All current inhabitants of the seven Planets of Thías, except those of Hunum, have already surpassed the Third Dimension of consciousness, and its inhabitants only return there to help, although most do not like the idea of returning to worlds where cruelty, selfishness, and fear still exist. In summary, the decision is an act of sublime Love and great courage. It means going to the aid of your younger siblings, being born under the same conditions, without awareness of who you are or what you have to do, with no other defense than your own internal advancement."

Mae-uhkel watched as the guide took another floating sphere, and they instantly found themselves in another place and time on the same planet Zax, zaxeans thías after the episode at the Center of Illumination. They were inside a vast, amber-colored temple; its golden, angle-less doors, its walls, and ceilings carefully decorated with organic figures as if part of the same Creation, achieved a seamless balance between the building and nature. Beautiful crystals and precious stones arranged specifically seemed to channel energies from higher planes, making for a sublime spectacle. Additionally, a pleasant scent of wildflowers filled the air with tranquil harmony; the beautiful building itself was an astonishing experience of light, scent, and color, simply inviting one to stay. The Love and Peace of the place were almost tangible.

"This is the headquarters of the Kjacam-Khuba" said the Guide.

"JaKu... what?" asked Mae-uhkel.

"Kjacam-Khuba, they are the Lovers of Wisdom, representatives of The Wisdom that Act for Love. It's a council composed of twenty-one Gaemas, as you have called them, with a long journey through time and therefore belonging to the High Evolutionary Dimensions from the Fifth, and guides of these worlds."

"Guides? But everyone here seems to be perfect beings, not needing to be guided by anyone."

"Well, no, there is always room to grow, and the beings of the Fourth Dimension are not the exception. They have things to learn and overcome, but yes, they have already achieved a society where Love, Wisdom, and Will reign in balance. Then they continue working on individual perfection and contact with the Master Mind and the development of the creative power..."

"The Master Mind" mused Mae-uhkel "Of course, now I understand more the first Law of the Tablets, how did it go? Ah yes, THE ALL IS MIND; the universe is mental. Everything occurs first in the mind. This is the power of powers, the source of every miraculous work in the whole world..."

"Exactly Mae-uhkel, remember in your religion it's said, ' created in his image and likeness ', that's what it refers to, we are all creators. From the third dimension, when we leave the animal kingdom and become aware of our individuality, we start creating; first our own realities and as we perfect ourselves in mastering our power, we advance to the Fourth, Fifth, Sixth Dimension and beyond; guides of worlds, creators of worlds, galaxies, and universes always growing towards the Master Mind. But watch, that one about to speak is the Wise Adelín," it said, pointing to the center of the main hall.

"Oh yeah, It's the same one we saw earlier at the Center of Illumination."

"That's right, he's a very wise and ancient Kjacam-Khuba. He also holds the position of Lumier, a great responsibility to show the way, requiring significant advancement and profound humility and service to his peers.

"As we know, the fraternity of this Thía system belonging to the Great Brotherhood of Worlds are largely committed to the growth of our younger sibling Hunum. Planet Hunum, the third of the seven of Thía, has lagged in its evolution, due to the hunumanity inhabiting it, causing a delay in the growth of not just the Thía System but the entire galaxy.

*https://opensea.io/collection/another-world-the-book*

Adelín stood before five beings in the center of the great hall, explaining to them:

*https://opensea.io/collection/another-world-the-book*

Although it's time for it to ascend to the Fourth Dimension, it remains in the Third and, despite many of its inhabitants awakening from their long sleep of unconsciousness, their leaders, strategically positioned and led by the darkness of selfishness, continue to exploit their lowest instincts and keep them ignorant of being children of the One, thus remaining at the head of a hunumanity torn between Light and shadow on its long evolutionary path. Among all the young volunteers, you five have been chosen by our Kjacam-Khubas. Khalil from Planet Volux, second of Thía..." As the wise named them, a three-dimensional hologram with all their information appeared, allowing Mae-uhkel to recognize them. Their faces were familiar, though he couldn't fathom why.

"Lover of Science as an expression of the Divine, Ooremis from Kalwais; sharp-minded and with a masterful knowledge of the Power of the Word, Pawqar of fiery spirit; analytical and from the World of Justice in Thía, Jurus... The Zaxian Fahel, possessing great determination and strength and, finally, a wise spirit that we all embraced as one of our small children, today an inhabitant of Zax but originally from Hunum, who had the vision and courage to make conscious efforts to develop Love and grow towards the One, beyond what is normal for his planet siblings, thus earning a place among us today, after being rescued from a massive extinction event on his home planet... My Beloved Gheldar..."

At that moment, Mae-uhkel felt himself fading, looking at his Guide questioning:

"My Gheldar? that's how you greeted me upon arrival here, am I that, But...?" He was puzzled, wondering what it all meant. The guide smiled.

"What you'll see will give you clarity" and with a gesture invited him to continue paying attention to what was happening.

"You five have been selected for being the most strengthened in your faculties. It will be on this planet where you must arrive to prevent a catastrophe that would greatly impact the attempts of the Light to elevate the hunumans to the highest possible level, plunging them into a war of planetary proportions that would lead to a spiral of terror and suffering, making them easy prey for the dark facet. Hunum's evolutionary stagnation would mean the stagnation of the entire galaxy, which would be inconvenient.

Many of us are currently on service missions, incarnated or not, in Hunum. The light is advancing, but the members of the shadows are also doing their job to stop this advance, and the battle is increasingly fierce. The current situation is rapidly converging, in the following hunuman cycles, to lead population to a fratricidal war conflict, which could even affect our octaves if their aberrant nuclear weapons are used, leaving us no option but to act directly. The most powerful country in Hunum, known as Z-suní, has been developed as a tool by the planet's ruling elites for dominance and control over its hunumanity; it is led by beings who work for the shadows, some consciously and others unconsciously of who they are. The conscious ones know of the possibility of war and its consequences in each Dimension; hence they do not rest in their attempts to disturb us and have all their invisible armies constantly working. The unconscious ones, blinded by ambition and manipulated as puppets through their lower instincts, are the ones running that world. They keep their inhabitants enslaved without their knowledge. It is a world managed and controlled by their monstrous corporations and institutions and called 'financial' in charge of managing and expanding their immense wealth, including Hunum's fossil fuel Sápea, medical drugs, food, arms factories, and media and communication outlets. These elites believe they would greatly benefit from a war against the country of Deilgohu, rich in Sápea, some seizing its deposits, others enriching by selling weapons to both sides during the war, and the media spreading all that horror. Our mission is to send you to incarnate to prevent all this and ensure that Hunum's smooth and normal ascension is not interrupted. The plan designed by the Kjacam-Khubas along with your guides is as follows. You will take bodies in Hunum. From today until you leave, you will each be prepared to assume your role. As you might have noticed, all of you know each other from previous lives, arranged this way so that, once in Hunum, the Law of Vibration allows you to naturally feel affinity and approach each other. Four of you will be born in the country of Akuahgrandia, a herald of Peace, Freedom, and Justice in Hunum and mediator in the conflict. The fifth will be born in Lukón, a country of the race of the children of Amaterasu and leading in planetary technological and scientific advancement but will reside in Akuahgrandia in adulthood. That will be you, Khalil; the plan is for you to dedicate yourself to what you do best, science with consciousness. You'll bring an unknown clean energy source to the hunumans, a major solution to end the war attempts, replacing Sápea and benefiting all inhabitants of the planet. We tried these two cycles ago, but it failed. Our people were silenced, and their research disappeared. This time, we are sending a team. Ooremis, you will be working as an informatist, responsible for informing the masses. Your main mission will be to publicize Khalil's advanced experiments and prevent them from being silenced. Mae-uhkel suddenly, as if a light had illuminated his thought "Nissu!!!" he said, recognizing the Kalwaisian in the personality of the beautiful informatist, Nissa Berdat from Hunum.

"And how am I going to get into the communication networks, currently in the hands of the shadows?" Ooremis asked.

"Good question, that is why there will be Fahel, who will be born close to the one holding the reins of the main global news network, will ensure your entry into the channel and the dissemination of your information. In the other hand, we need someone in the plane, with enough power over society, to bring the technology to the people, to the masses, and that's where Pawqar comes in. You, with several incarnations as a great diplomat, will easily reach the presidency in Akuahgrandia to implement true politics and thus place Khalil at the forefront of the Eco Synthesis massification project."

During the entire speech, Gheldar listened silently, but then said:

"It seems like a perfect plan, but I don't understand my role. It looks like everything needed is covered."

"You're mistaken, my young friend" Adelín replied. "You are the glue of the structure and will have the most difficult task. As you know, upon incarnating in the third dimension, beings do not remember who they are or what they have to do. In a world as darkened and disconnected as Hunum currently is, it's very easy to remain ignorant of who they are, relying only on the inaudible voice of the One and their previous achievements. Due to your extensive development as a channel for clairvoyance and clairaudience in physical worlds, you'll have the ability to pierce the veil that covers most hunumans and discover who you are, who your companions are, what you're here to achieve, and make them aware of it. But remember that they won't recognize you so they might not believe you, and also it won't be easy to reach them."

"And why that last condition?" he interjected.

"In a world as Hunum, they still see each other separated by several aspects, social classes is one the main ones. You will belong to a class where scarcity is a daily struggle. Because it's necessary for your living conditions to be harsh, focusing your attention from a young age on internal cultivation, having the need to advance and grow very alive in yourself, so you can awaken to who you are as soon as possible. Now retire to your dwellings, consult with your Inner Self, and if you're here at dawn, it'll be a sign that you accept the mission, and only then will your preparation begins. But remember, it's not just about your near future, but the role to play for a population that needs you without knowing it and will surely resist being helped, as it has so many times before, condemning its saviors to suffering and even death, and exalting its tormentors to delirium. Love, Wisdom, and Will, and may the Light of the One always envelop you.

When Adelín speech finalized, Mae-uhkel asked his Guide:

"I realized I knew the girl from a few thías ago, but all their faces, not just hers, seem familiar to me. Why?'"

"You five are what some call soulmates. A group of beings with a similar evolutionary level and thousands of cycles incarnating together, as family, friends, teachers and students, on multiple planets, triumphing and being defeated, but always loving each other because that is the main reason for existence."

After the session, the volunteers looked at each other. In their faces, questions, excitement, and even a bit of joy could be read, knowing they were chosen for such an important task. As they left the building, they met informally:

"Gheldar, The Great Gheldar! I knew you would volunteer for this," Fahel said, embracing the calm hunuman. Gheldar laughed in response and said:

"And I knew...'"

"I know…" Fahel interrupted his fellow neighbor and friend. "…that they would choose me too, right, my clairvoyant?"

*https://opensea.io/collection/another-world-the-book*

"Well… no, what I was going to say is that I knew you would wear that outfit today… because you always wear the same one around this time every cycle… ha, ha, ha, ha!" They both laughed.

"These two! They live on the same planet and hug as if they never see each other" joked Ooremis, embracing both.

Khalil and Pawqar joined the fraternal greeting.

"What do you think of the mission?" Pawqar asked the group.

"It's hard to give an opinion right away without thinking it through," Khalil replied. 'However, we know that things in Hunum are not easy. How many of us are there now, tied to the plane?"

"Thousands," Ooremis answered.

"And worse, some have even joined the other side," Fahel commented, referring to the beings who had decided to incarnate to help and were now serving the shadows.

"Yes!" Ooremis and Pawqar exclaimed together.

"It's true that it's difficult, but I'm pretty sure we will go and succeed," Gheldar intervened.

"Well, that gives me more confidence coming from you, Gheldar," said Fahel, "because you see a little bit further than us."

"Not always," Gheldar replied.

"Okay, okay, I think we're delving too deeply into the topic without having consulted with The Principal Advisor," said Ooremis, pointing to her heart. "So, let's go home, and when Thía rises, we'll see what each of us decided; see you, dear friends, extremely happy to know I'd be with you once again. Love, Wisdom, and Will to all… and may the Light of the One illuminate us in our decision."

"Likewise, see you!" they all said and left. The two spectators returned to the Archive Hall.

# CHAPTER V

## BEFORE BIRTH

Instantly, as the Guide took the third sphere, they found themselves outside the Kjacam-Khubas headquarters.

"It's the next thía in Zax," the Guide informed Mae-uhkel. Gheldar was already sitting under a tree, writing in his qelca, just like Mae-uhkel did daily in his notebook, waiting for the rest of the group. The quite dawn was broken by the voice of Ooremis:

"Thías shines beautifully, perfect to start our training. I thought I'd be the first to arrive, but it seems you never went home, Gheldar."

Right behind Khalil expressed: "Greetings of Love, Wisdom, and Will to my future hunuman companions, well, to two of them because I see we're not all here yet... or are we? I hope not!"

"Welcome, my friends," Gheldar responded to both. Shortly after, they were surrounded by a magenta energy of Love and Gratitude from Pawqar, who greeted them silently, just sending his energy from the heart. "And Fahel?" he asked upon arrival.

"He hasn't arrived yet," Ooremis answered.

"But it's time to get in, do you know if he'll come?" Pawqar inquired, starting to head towards the Kjacam-Khuba Hall, followed by the others.

Suddenly, Fahel materialized right in their path, surprising everyone.

"Were you going to Hunum without me?" he asked with a smile, and they all embraced him.

"That was exactly what we didn't want," Gheldar said, playfully ruffling Fahel's hair.

"Sorry for being late, but I had things to do. Let's go, they're waiting for us… because of me, of course," he said, gently pulling Ooremis by the arm.

"How did he just appear out of nowhere?" Mae-uhkel asked.

'Beings of the Fourth Dimension can disintegrate and integrate their bodies at will within the same evolutionary spheres or planets, as you call them."

"Then why do they walk?" Mae-uhkel wondered.

"They also know the benefits of daily exercise and connecting with nature and their peers. They walk because they truly enjoy and benefit from it."

"And what about all those ships?"

"Only from the Fifth Dimension onwards can beings teleport to other planets and dimensions. Those of the Fourth need their ships for that."

In the Main Hall, Mae-uhkel saw his guide sitting next to the twenty-one Sages and other Beautiful Beings.

"Is that you? Were you there at that time?" Mae-uhkel asked his Guide.

"I have always been with you, My Gheldar," the Guide replied, transforming into a playful Harlequin, touching Mae-uhkel deeply.

"So, you were Hoyín, my invisible friend from my childhood!"

"Yes, I am the representative of the One for you. Every being can have a guide. Remember the beings next to the ruffians in the fight? they were their guides too."

"But why didn't they defend them?"

"Because Love is also respect. Respect for free will. Their Guides wanted to help, but they never were asked for it, the hunumans were remaining stubborn in their violence.'

"Why didn't I see you as I grew up?"

"It's not entirely true," the Guide said, transforming into different people that he didn't recognize until finally he assumed the shape of the young huno who had once asked Mae-uhkel for directions. "My most direct actions were in your moments of greatest need and least clarity. When you're most distracted from yourself, that's when you can least see and hear beyond your physical senses."

Now in the Main Hall, the Kjacam-Khubas, the Guides of each volunteer, and Other High Intelligences were all seated on the main platform. The tallest of them all, with magenta hair, violet eyes, and a look of sublime closeness to Divinity, stood up and introduced herself to the five chosen ones:

*https://opensea.io/collection/another-world-the-book*

"May the Light of the One always illuminate you, and may Divine Virtues cover your paths throughout Eternity, Children of Thías! I am Amina, Messiah of Hunum, and I bear the primary responsibility for the destiny of all those sparks that, though they emanate from the heart of the One, have, since their origins, debated between Light and shadow up until now. Many cycles ago, my messianic mission led me directly to Hunum. Nine times I took on flesh, being born as a hunuman during nine distinct periods in the history of that school sphere—times when darkness seemed to prevail. Yet, with the support of many of you and other valuable beings, we lifted that humanity, guiding it back to the Mother-Father.

"Nine times, the Flame of Truth was rekindled to illuminate the path, but those nine incarnations were each extinguished, slain by unconsciousness and incomprehension. Nevertheless, after my departure, all of you—my companions, followers, helpers, and disciples—remained on the plane, continuing to spread the Light in the darkness. Yet time and again, you were persecuted, besieged, and annihilated, and our message was mutilated, altered, and distorted, resulting in the various hunuman religions. Nine lives, nine religions. Religions born of division, conflict and war. Religions of deception and domination. Nothing could be further from the nature of our Father-Mother, who is Oneness, who is Love, and who is Peace.

The Eternal Law no longer allows me to answer the call of my heart that urges me to be there with them, to rescue them with my own hands. That is why" she said, turning to the panel "my eternal gratitude goes to you, my brethren, for in my physical absence, you carry out this beautiful and commendable work of aid. It is well known that those who give more will receive more, and thus, each of you will receive a thousandfold all the Love you have bestowed upon your sibling Hunum, who, being the youngest, is the last to accept the greatness of the Uncreated Light and thereby join the concert of Elevated Worlds, which, by overcoming their baseness through Will, conquered Love, Wisdom, and Truth."

Turning her gaze again to the chosen five and with a look of infinite Love, she continued, "Now, the Supreme Intelligence, which is Light and Whole Compassion, places you on this path that you have courageously accepted. You will be united and assisted by the thousands who serve Above and Below, and through them, my hands will touch where I can no longer reach, and my feet will walk where I can no longer tread. But even so, I will always be with you, in that silent voice that knows no boundaries of Dimension or time. Go, worthy children of Thías, and may the Light of Gaemo, Father and Mother, be your sword and shield"

Moved to tears, Mae-uhkel felt a newfound strength within. He had awoken to who he was and what he needed to do. The Messiah's words were etched in his heart and in those of the group, a testament to what they left behind to rescue their siblings from their own ignominy.

The five chosen were surrounded by their group of Guides, leading them to different rooms to plan the details. Located in their respective rooms, each volunteer was seated on a 'dense air couch,' a kind of translucent cloud supported by five electrodes. Lying there, seemingly floating, the chosen ones, accompanied by their Guides, began to delve into the details of each life.

The chief Guide of each volunteer led the session. The future incarnate faced a device with seven light appendages, each directed towards an energy point along the body, from the head to the spine's end. This setup allowed perceiving vibrations and details of all presented information. Before the session began, with concentration, everyone energized the space to achieve the highest elevation possible for making the best decisions. The final decision, of course, respected absolute Free Will and was voluntarily and consciously made by the being itself. A deep voice that seems to come from nowhere and everywhere said:Gheldar de Falguem, native of Hunum but a refugee in Zax, belonging to the Magenta Hosts of Love. As a legionnaire of this beautiful quality of the Mother-Father, you have defended and expanded it, even at the cost of your own life in multiple incarnations.

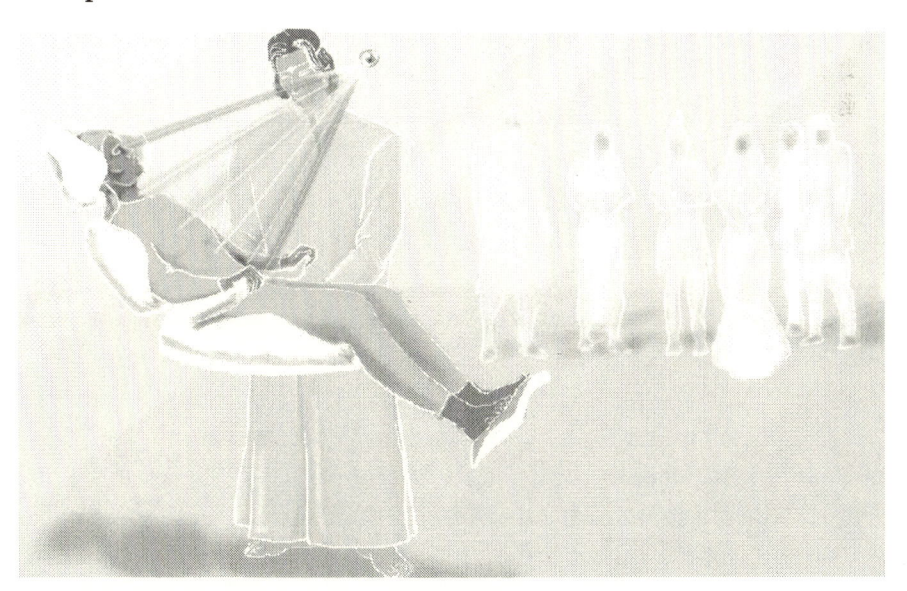

*https://opensea.io/collection/another-world-the-book*

A great seeker of Wisdom and Truth; your weakness, being a being of Love, tends towards naivety and sometimes lacks the Will to do what is necessary. Therefore, we recommend your birth on the first thía in the hunuman Fifths, when this quality of Will is most energized. We also suggest the hunuman name of Mae-uhkel, whose sound strengthens this virtue with its vibration. The following families we will present to you are all in tune with your vibration, known to you throughout your long journey through eternity, during your various incarnations. Of all of them, we can suggest three, which will be the most suitable to carry out the Mission entrusted to you, however, the final decision will be yours."

The Guide fell silent, allowing Gheldar to internalize each option. After pondering the data for a while and focusing internally, he seemed decided. The Granahoi Family was his choice, one of the three suggested by the Council. "I am pleased to see you considered our suggestion. It is a wise choice," the Guide communicated mentally, placing his hand on Gheldar's shoulder.

The Granahoi family, composed only of the Granahoi spouses at the time, would welcome Mae-uhkel as the third member and only child. His future parents, both originally from Hunum, were not strangers to him; she had been his sister in a past life, hence her love for him. She had also achieved a level of growth towards the One, superior to her hunuman peers, similar to Gheldar. She would be his great ally and support during his childhood, in facing the harsh conditions of the plane and protecting him from the hostile environment in which he would grow. His father, on the other hand, had been his companion and friend in a previous incarnation in Hunum, when both were students in an initiatic school of that remote past. Although life had taken them on different paths, and the development of knowledge and psychic abilities achieved by this being, sadly, had been used for disharmonious purposes during that and subsequent incarnations, acting as his father now would provide the future body of Mae-uhkel the genetic base necessary for the development of his abilities upon birth in Hunum.

After finalizing details like the date of incarnation and exact location, among others, Gheldar's long session ended. After notifying his Zaxian relatives and friends of his upcoming Mission, he began the Conjunction, preparing for the birth of the hunuman baby that would be animated by Gheldar, the loving, the clairvoyant, the one in charge of awakening his mission brothers.

The last sphere shown by the guide to Mae-uhkel appeared to be a hunuman medical office. Looking around, he saw his much younger, pregnant mother sitting in front of the Munai's desk. Mae-uhkel listened to their conversation.

"Everything is ready, Galera Granahoi. This is the birth date according to the pregnancy time, but the baby seems quite ready, and we could move it along," said the obstetrician. In Mae-uhkel's clear state, thanks to his recent experiences, he noticed details that most overlooked. The Munai, in his need for efficiency and pragmatism, wanted to perform a cesarean section on what would be his mother. The normal birthing process involved much more time and dedication, making it, in his view, inefficient, less profitable, and unnecessarily risky. In this last criterion, the fear factor, dominant in worlds like Hunum, was a decisive factor. What the doctor failed to realize was that Nature, in its perfection, created processes as their purpose warranted. The journey of the newborn through the pelvic canal provides physiological and psychological benefits in the child's future development. Sadly, general medicine in Hunum was ignorant of all this. Mae-uhkel's future mother didn't understand what her Munai was trying to tell her:

"How is that, Munai Swan?"

"I'll explain, Galera. Our facilities are full for the quint you're scheduled for, but we have spots for the earlier quint. Don't worry, there's no problem, it's the same, and the baby can be born now if he's ready."

"Well, why not let him be born when is his time?" asked Galera Granahoi, feeling the Munai's attitude kind of uncomfortable.

"The main reason is what I just told you. Also, it will be a cesarean delivery because your pelvis is very narrow...".

The Munai then extended a convoluted and complex medical explanation, concluding with, "We shouldn't risk a natural birth and risk the baby coming on a thía when there's no space, facing a serious emergency that endangers both of your lives. It's better and safer to plan everything."

Mae-uhkel's mother fell silent and nodded her head, having no choice but to silently accept the 'medical authority.'

After this scene, Mae-uhkel returned to Zax and observed Gheldar, eyes closed, lying in a brightly lit, immaculate white room. Suddenly, he felt a strange but pleasant sensation. It was like merging with Gheldar, both in one body, but then abruptly and violently 'torn' from the contemplative state he was in. He felt cold and fear. He was born in Hunum, unnaturally, as the baby Granahoi, on the first thía of the previous quint, due to the 'wise advice' of the Munai in charge.

*https://opensea.io/collection/another-world-the-book*

# CHAPTER VI
## FOLLOWING THE THREAD

That thía Mae-uhkel woke up renewed, having – reborn – , feeling unstoppable and capable of anything. He thanked Gaemo, The Universal Mind, and with a strong desire to connect, sat on his bed and closed his eyes, meditating for a while. Upon opening them, he noticed a lump beside him – someone was sleeping next to him! Carefully, he approached to see who it was, noticing faint threads of light connecting him to the sleeping figure. It was a Bham-yi of Laziness and Drowsiness that made him want to stay in bed every morning and sometimes even prevented him from fulfilling his duties.

As Mae-uhkel practiced his connection, deepened self-control and abilities, his vision stayed awake longer. The existence of the Bham-yi made him smile sheepishly, then he closed his eyes again and, with a deep breath, decided to try what he had learned—or remembered. He concentrated a violet-hued point of light that grew into a toroidal shape, then the energy emerged from his heart, enveloping the curious entity, He understood Bham-yis were beings created because of something we had been needing for a long time. In that state of mind was clear to him that he needs to pay more attention to himself and try to rest more, sleeping and practicing his connection routine more often. When this thought crossed his mind, the Banhyi slowly vanished along with its sensations

of heaviness and drowsiness. Surprised by his newfound ability, he went straight to write it down along with all the other information he had received during his dream. Then on his wall, he set out to identify his mission companions, looking at the list of people he had already written down. Nissa was the first he highlighted. He also had Galek on his list of Visible Bright Beings, whom he had seen in the channel with his brilliant heart walking through the corridors carefree and happy. He had even exchanged a few words with him; he was like a fresh breeze in the midst of the usual atmosphere in the RB area; moreover, he was struck by the fact that he, even being the son of the magnate Zoren Zics, was an accessible person, showed no social conventionalism and on the contrary, was simple and friendly. He identified in him the Zaxian Fahel. He only had Pawqar, a diplomat from Jurus, and the scientist Khalil left, but he knew where to start. Mae-uhkel noted: Pawqar – presidential candidate – and Khalil and next to it the phrase – Eco Synthesis – . Then he dressed and dashed out, not without first saying goodbye to his mother who was still in her room, with a shout.

" Good morning, Mom, see you later and… by the way" he said already on his way out, while tying his shoes "you shouldn't have listened to the Munai and accepted my cesarean section. Gaemo is perfect and one quint later, when it really corresponded to me, surely there would have been a bed for you" and he left leaving his mother astonished and confused. He immediately went to tell Leyhana about his experience, he couldn't wait to get there, surely they would have a lot to talk about. But when he left his house and looked over the balcony in the hallway, he was stunned, both realities were in full splendor there, mixed into one. Energies of colors emerged not only from people but from EVERYTHING, animals, plants, rocks and all looked connected, he saw how these traveled and were shared by everything in a synchronous dance of energetic exchanges; people walked folloved by their Bham-yis, some of them looked like – hibernating – probably satiated, others clearly active, hungry, demanding energy or absorbing it from their creators. People accompanied by Gaemas, others by Tumsas, others that seemed to be protected by Gaemas from the influence of Tumsas who in turn tried to reach themwith suggestions but were dissolved in the air, before reaching the mental field of the being. Also a few disincarnate individuals, some wandering, others next to incarnates just accompanying them or trying desperately to make some kind of contact. In short, beings and energies visible and invisible coexisting…

*https://opensea.io/collection/another-world-the-book*

And it had always been like that: what manifests in the visible world has its origin in the invisible world, where the true causes reside, Mae-uhkel thought while setting out for Leyhana's house. When he arrived at the floor where his friend lived, he was surprised that the old huna did not foresee his arrival and open the door for him before he knocked, as she usually did. He rang the bell and knocked on the door, for the first time, but she did not answer. Maybe she had gone out or maybe she didn't hear, or something worse? This last thought caused him anxiety and disconnected him, his enlightenment faded. He made a third, somewhat stronger than normal attempt, already

worried, but in case his friend didn't hear. The neighbor from the next apartment responded to the noise:

"Can I help you with something?"

"Good morning, I'm looking for Galera Leyhana, have you seen her today?"

"Excuse me, who are you looking for?" the neighbor inquired again.

"Galera Leyhana, the old huna next door."

"You must have the wrong address, young huno."

"No, please, the elderly from this apartment, she's my friend, come on, she's your neighbor!" he said desperately while gesturing with his arms, highlighting the proximity of both doors.

"You must be mistaken, friend, that apartment has been unoccupied for over a cycle now" he emphasized, closing the door with a disdainful look at such a crazy claim. Mae-uhkel was bewildered; he tried to peek through the gap under the door, but saw no movement. How could this be possible? For a brief moment, he doubted himself and everything that had happened. He ran down to the concierge and asked the doorman who replied:

"Yes, the one for sale?" when Mae-uhkel referred to the location of the dwelling.

"Uh, yes, I guess…" he said quickly but still confused about the situation, then he thought to ask

"How long has it been unoccupied? Do you know the owners' names?"

"About a cycle, yes, it's a young couple, foreigners, I think" Mae-uhkel pondered and then asked again. "You said it's for sale, right? Could you show it to me?"

"Sure, just a moment…" The concierge took the key and went with him to the apartment.

Indeed. To his total surprise, it was completely empty and dusty. It certainly looked like it had been that way for a long time. Mae-uhkel quickly went through it, realizing this. Finally, disheartened and realizing there was nothing more to see, he left and sat on the stairs in front of the door to think about what was going on. He was utterly bewildered. After reviewing everything he had experienced, it couldn't be, something wasn't right.

Sitting there on the stairs, Mae-uhkel began to question everything, again. Had he imagined it all? The conversations, the moments of clarity, her guiding presence—were they mere fabrications of a mind slipping into madness, like his father before him? The emptiness of the apartment gnawed at him, the silence deafening, as if the very walls mocked his uncertainty. Maybe he was losing his grip on reality, and everything he had clung to for solace was just a mirage, a desperate attempt to hold onto his sanity.

A little while of doubting and spiraling deeper into despair made him remember, somehow, his dream, the words of the Messiah, and what he had learned with Leyhana. He decided to try it, took a deep breath, as an attempt to calm down, as she had taught him. In that moment of connection, the convolution in his mind stopped, and a sense of peace began to settle over him, allowing to pause his internal turmoil and see things more clearly.

Suddenly, he looked up and noticed the peculiar handmade plaque with the numbers indicating the apartment number; he went back in and asked the doorman: "Excuse me, why is this plaque different from the rest?"

"Oh, it's nothing. I just decided to change it recently; the old one was deteriorating."

"Hmm, and why did you use that particular design and not the same as the others?

"You know what, good question, I don't really know, this is a very old building, you know, those are not available anymore, that design came to my mind and I made it that way, but if you don't like it, you can change it."

"No, it's fine, I was just curious" he said suspiciously while going out again to sit on the stairs in front of the door but now with his eyes on the curious plate, he thought, could it be a projected idea? Then he looked at it closely and this time more carefully, he stood up from the step that served as an improvised seat and with a gesture of curiosity, took the perie[21] number from above and turned it…

---

21   Perie: Hunum's number in Akuahgrandian language

*https://opensea.io/collection/another-world-the-book*

"BUT OF COURSE, THAT'S IT! – He had realized it couldn't be a coincidence... How had he not seen it before? The perie number upside down with the other two and screws in both sides, all in silver, formed 'The Symbol' from his dreams, his guide, the Council... at that moment the doorman came out about to close the door and telling him:

"Well, you saw it, what do you think? The plaque is no problem I tell you..." However, Mae-uhkel prevented him from closing the door with his foot and interrupted him excitedly.

"Wait, one last look please!" he exclaimed, grabbing the door and going back in, he stopped in the center of the dwelling and slowly went over his steps in the head, all that he had done the previous thía with Leyhana and then in the spot where he had sat and learned the contact exercise, his attention was drawn to a crumpled paper thrown in a corner next to him. As he approached to see it, he noticed in one corner of the small sheet the handwritten phrase: 'The ALL is...', he bent down and picked it up...

*https://opensea.io/collection/another-world-the-book*

He was thrilled, it was the paper Leyhana wrote with the laws he had read, but he also noticed that at the end of the paper there was a note of a text that did not belong to the Quam-Rú Tablets and that he had not seen before: "Remember, I´m ALWAYS with you, My brave Gheldar!" His skin tingled remembering: 'My most direct actions were in your moments of greatest need and least clarity. When you're most distracted from yourself, that's when you can least see and hear beyond your physical senses.

"Oh, my Gaemo! I was coming from the chapel the thía I met her!" Mae-uhkel exclaimed with tears on his eyes and a wide smile draw on his face.

Leyhana had always been his Guide...there again. Closing his eyes and with his hand on his chest he expressed a heartfelt "Thank you My Leyhana!" and ran out leaving the voice of the doorman behind who yelled to him:

"So… did you like it?... Let me know then if you are interested and please say it was me who showed it to you!"

"I will, thank you so much sir!" he shouted as he crossed the stairs on his way up.

Back in his house, he only had one thought in his head: to find the missionaries he had yet to identify. However, he didn't know where to start. Politics was not a topic in which Mae-uhkel had been much involved, but Science was, so there is where he started. He searched for Eco Synthesis and those who were currently working on it. He discovered the story of what had happened, indeed and as he remembered in the dream, two scientists published having achieved it with positive results. When asked to repeat the experiment, they were not able to, they said they needed more time to determine the variables that intervened and to be able to reproduce the exact conditions again, but it was too late. The scientific community vilified and discredited them. They lost resources and research was stopped. Inquiring he discovered a whole campaign of discrediting and hiding information against the two chemists, but nothing more about them, their subsequent research or their whereabouts after the incident. History had swallowed them. He reached the notes of his dream and reviewing them he remembered Adelín's words: "…We already tried these two cycles ago, but it was unsuccessful. Ours were silenced and their investigations disappeared…" He continued his investigation and obtained information about a group in the country of Lukón that had made some progress. It was not very abundant and lacked names and details, but he remembered that Khalil would be born in Lukón and this made him think that there he might be…

He looked information about Lukon and when he saw all the images and scenes, his attention got caught on it's the technological magnificence. Admiring the advances of Lukon and its society, he started comparing and thinking about its differences with his country, Akuahgrandia, and this brought his attention back to the political aspect of his journey… but he didn't know much about it. Like in most countries in Hunum, that beautiful discipline that sought to govern the organization of peoples with freedom and justice through the participation and contribution of each of its members in society, for the common advancement and growth, was completely distorted and perverted. It became instead a twisted tool of domination, in which through ignorance, fear, and frivolity, they had turned the majority into unconscious defenders of their own oppressors. In summary, the strategy of those who held political-economic power was let the population be occupied with entertainment, sports, celebrity culture, and consumption, and leave to us the important things: the command of society and its affairs… The final result was that the majority were not greatly interested and for many others, politics was synonymous with corruption. The remaining few who were interested were mostly either direct beneficiaries of the current governments or simply naive believers. Mae-uhkel was not immune to this reality and was among those who scorned the importance of true politics out of ignorance. He knew that at some point four candidates competed and that the polls indicated that Sekk Ragner, the candidate of the official party, was leading, and that he had a conservative stance. Then, far below in the polls, the main opposition party to the fraction in power, was an Openness Party, Labor Party, with a candidate named Keto. Third and fourth were two more candidates with a few points, one of quasi- openness and an independent, whose names he did not remember. He then opened his old proccuan[22] ready to identify the one from Jurus among them. He was surprised to realize that the electoral panorama had changed a lot since the last time he saw any news about it, conjunctions ago. The current contest was between the official candidate, Munai Sekk Ragner and the independent Kelia Zaver, although the former doubled her advantage according to conventional media.

*https://opensea.io/collection/another-world-the-book*

"Look at this candidate, she has risen like foam" he thought, but the decision was obvious and as his first option he chose the most popular candidate. He looked up his resume, a very academically prepared huno,

---

22   Hunuman equivalent of a portable personal computer

with Munaide and Postmunaide in two of the best Major Schools of Z-Suní and a long career in the People's Will party, currently and for five cycles in power in Akuahgrandia, occupying different positions within the party. He looked for several interviews on the net. Mae-uhkel, who was not very versed in the subject, thought it was fine and thought that perhaps it could be Pawqar. He proposed to try to approach him in person to contact him and try to carry out his work. So he sent the information to his nokó and went to the channel with the intention of contacting Galek.

He arrived and was pleasantly surprised to see Nissa who was in the corridors.

"Hello Mae-uhkel, good afternoon"

"Wow galera Nissu! how are you? Nice to see you here, tell me what happened with you?"

"It's Nissa!..." "my dear COWORKER," she said emphatically showing her new badge and then added notoriously excited "I am a Research Informatist...and please, stop treating me formally, remember? Where were you that I hadn't seen you around?"

"What!?, Oh that's great, ma'am! I mean, Nissa..." he hurried to correct himself but, at the same time, seemed overexcited about Nissa's news. Of course, she was oblivious to everything that fact meant to him. However, Mae-uhkel realized this too and, to tone things down a little, he added, "...and yes, I have been absent; I am on vacation until a few days from now. I had several days accumulated and decided to take them all at once..." he made a pause and then continued "Oh, so, now that you mention your job, Nissa, it occurs to me that maybe you could help me with something..."

"Oh, sure, please tell me."

"No, not here. It's a bit long to tell and it's also personal. Do you think we can meet somewhere else? – This proposal seemed a bit daring to Mae-uhkel for someone he had barely met, and even more so after seeing her reluctant face when he said that. However, knowing already who she was, he decided to use his new ability to energize the virtue of Love in Nissa.; he did it, similarly to how he had done it in his bed with the Bham-yi, he concentrated on his heart, breathed deeply and a magenta-colored spiral of energy covered him like a sphere and then grew until it touched Nissa's heart completely enveloping her as well.

*https://opensea.io/collection/another-world-the-book*

The beautiful informatist felt a fraternal love for the young huno and a desire to help him, which led her to smile and respond almost without thinking: "Of course, Mae-uhkel coincidentally today I have nothing to do after work, and I also owe you one... If you want, we can meet and talk"

"Perfect!" Mae-uhkel replied. "We'll meet at Shazaá Lombardo, do you know it? "

"Yes, in the Shopping Garden?"

"Exactly, see you there then, at the end of the thía, thank you very much Nissa."

Mae-uhkel was excited, everything was going according to plan and also... it had worked!!! He felt like a superhero with new powers in mission. He smiled at that thought but immediately heard in his head the voice of Leyhana, his guide: "To whom much is given, much will be demanded"

Mae-uhkel blushed, but at the same time, rejoiced to hear his friend again and squeezed his heart remembering that she had always been and would always be with him.

However, at the same time, darkness was also doing its work, and at Galek's house, one of the Hunuman members of the service staff was preparing breakfast when a Tumsa suggested she watch – the interesting interview – with the musical group of the moment being broadcasted right then. She rushed to turn on the RB, leaving the kitchen gas open, which caused the fire alarm to go off. The firefighters came to the house, and the commotion caused by this series of unexpected events – coincidentally – delayed Galek that thía, preventing Mae-uhkel from contacting him that afternoon to pave the way for his awakening. He could wait no longer; it was time for his meeting with Nissa.

Finally, when Galek was about to head to the channel, a Tumsa took advantage of the low feelings of jealousy and envy harbored in the heart of Barhana, the perfect gateway to use him for their purposes. Galek's nokó rang:

"Hello dear, don't you love me anymore? You haven't called me for thías."

"Hello Barhi! Sorry, I've been very busy with my dad's stuff…"

"Yes, I imagine, but that's no reason to abandon me."

"Of course, is not, you're right."

"How is your dad?"

"The same. Stable, at least."

"He's going to get better, you'll see. By the way, changing the subject, I also know that you've been busy for another reason that you're not telling me."

"What are you talking about?"

"I heard that you were seen with Nissa Berdat, very, very cozy. Dear friend, I shouldn't tell you this, but I know her well from school years and she never gave me a good vibe. It was said about her that she was a libertine who was with everyone and no one." A vile comment from the jealous friend, who had always been in love with Galek, never managing to be seen by him as anything more than a good friend. "Besides, seeing her on the news made me feel I had to tell you. Galek, the one who gave her your nokóde was me. She called asking me to talk to you to see if there was a spot in the staff. I told her to call you herself, though now you were very upset with your dad's situation; I knew it wasn't the best time and also I thought she'd never dare… but apparently she did it and with success…"

*https://opensea.io/collection/another-world-the-book*

Galek was surprised and skeptical by the comment about Nissa, but on the other hand, Barhana had been his friend for a long time, and her word was important to him. "I don't know, I find it hard to believe. On the contrary, she hesitated to tell me that she had submitted her application for a position at the channel."

"Oh Galek, don't be naive! but in the end, she told you, right?"

"Well, yes."

"Oh, my love, clearly you don't know hunas… how sneaky we can be when we want something. We're the best actresses."

"Okay Barhi, I'll keep that in mind. I must leave because I'm driving, we'll talk later, bye now" He continued in his vehicle towards the channel, but now with the idea that the malicious Barhana had put in his mind. When Nissa arrived at Shazaá Lombardo, Mae-uhkel was already sitting at a table, writing in his notebook.

"Hello! I'm not late, am I?" she asked, looking at her nokó.

"No, not at all, I just came a bit earlier, was trying to organize my thoughts, please sit down" Mae-uhkel invited her.

"Okay, then tell me, how can I be of help? You've got me intrigued."

"Yes. As you told me that you're into investigative journalism, I thought you might be able to help me with a search I'm advancing. I'm studying

Applied Psychophysics and as part of my thesis project at the Major School, I'm researching Eco Synthesis, have you heard anything about that?"

"Not really, what is it?" asked an intrigued Nissa.

"It's a non-polluting, economical, and almost inexhaustible form of energy.

"Wow, sounds like an energy panacea."

"Yeah, kind of unbelievable, right? Well, it's a long story, but the important thing now is that is a real thing and there are few people in the world working on this today. It seems that a group in Lukón believes they have made interesting progress. However, I can't get enough information about them by my means, and I think I've exhausted them. That's where I need your help. I would like to contact these people to delve deeper into my work.

"Okay Mae-uhkel, I think through our correspondence in Lukón we could get information."

"But one more thing Nissa. I must advise you to be discreet. You should know, before deciding whether you want to help me, that the topic in the scientific world is a bit delicate due to a situation that occurred cycles ago with two researchers who were accused of being charlatans. The topic today is considered almost esoteric, taboo in academia. You should be cautious about your reputation when talking to other people, especially at the channel."

"Alright, I understand, and thanks for the heads up. Don't worry, I'll handle it with care."

"Yes, that's best."

They continued talking, fine-tuning details, and at that moment, Mae-uhkel thought that Nissa could also help him meet Munai Ragner, so he asked: "By the way, Nissa, do you know if there's any scheduled interview with Ragner at the channel in the coming thías? I would like to meet him."

"What? Are you serious? And why would you want to meet that old fogey?"

"Don't call him that," Mae-uhkel said, foreseeing that he might be the genius Pawqar. "He's a highly educated and well-regarded person."

"Come on Mae-uhkel…" she said, about to start an argument, but immediately regretted it and exclaimed resignedly: "Never mind. I have to go," she said as she collected her belongings from the table, visibly upset.

"No, please, Nissa. What's wrong?"

"Nothing, I just don't like to talk about the subject." Politics was a sensitive topic for Nissa, and she struggled to stay calm when someone contradicted her views without, in her opinion, valid arguments. Mae-uhkel noticed an abnormal passion in her when talking about the subject, however, thinking that his friend might be wrong and that, moreover, it was his duty to make her recognize the personality of the Jurusian in Ragner, he insisted: "No, please, let's talk."

"Okay, but only because you're asking me to. I think that he is nothing more than a representative of the status quo, a puppet they want to put there to ensure that nothing changes and things stay just as bad."

"Who are 'They' Nissa"

"The elites that really rule the world in the shadow…"

This comment grabs the attention of Mae-uhkel however he choose to say: "Well, remember that we never know who people can be internally, and we shouldn't judge them just by their political inclination or bias. Maybe Munai Ragner has good intentions."

"I don't think so and even if he does Mae-uhkel, intentions are not enough, it takes real will to generate the profound changes that our society requires. Ragner represents, in my opinion, those who look out for themselves, and we need someone who belongs to the side of those who care about all of us.

"Well, and if it's not Munai Ragner, who do you think it is? Because the rest are nobodies."

"It's not important who they are, what matters are the ideas they propose, there's Kelia Zaver, for example."

"What, that crazy huna's defender? Have you seen everything is said about her, Nissa?" Mae-uhkel was looking for Pawqar in the personality of one of the male candidates, which is why he had outright dismissed candidate Zaver Besides her reputation in public opinion was not the best. Nissa rolled her eyes obstinately and replied:

"Exactly Mae-uhkel, analyze a bit who is saying what they say about her. They are the media… "The ones you work for…" Mae-uhkel refuted.

"Sure, but they are Private Companies... they don't give space to new ideas, only the ones that suit them... I have to go, but Mae-uhkel, remember that the Truth is always at least one level deeper than what everyone believes they know" Nissa concluded as she got up from the table. Mae-uhkel remained seated, thoughtful, with his friend's ideas in his head.

After this conversation, he went to his proccuan. Based on the information he had, he believed that Ragner was Pawqar, but Nissa's words, "The Truth is at least one level deeper than what everyone thinks they know" made him reconsider. Thinking about this for a while, he decided to search for alternative information sources. Independent and unbiased sources, community media outlets, opened a different reality for him. Candidate Zaver appeared time and again, working with people, attending to the needy, involved in community issues. He found an interview with her on a small community RB station. Her speech was passionate, fiery, speaking of Love, Equality, and mutual aid; words that resonated in Mae-uhkel's heart. But he immediately scolded himself for being swayed by the candidate's message, deviating from his original plan to find Pawqar. He returned to his search, but found nothing.

Then, he remembered what he had learned with Leyhana, to look inside his heart... He lay down, breathed deeply, and focused on his chest, then he had a vision of a street with many people gathered, seemingly happy and celebrating. He managed to see a sign with the name – Tres Raíces Street – before the vision faded. Opening his eyes, he went to the proccuan and searched for 'Tres Raíces Street + candidate' and discovered it was the location of a meeting between candidate Zaver and the people of that community that very thía. Mae-uhkel was confused, he looked at the krono, didn't have much time to speculate, and decided simply to follow his vision and head to the location.

Arriving in the Tres Raíces Street neighborhood, people were gathered, waiting for the Nomocat's arrival with music and dances. There was a lot of joy and hope in the air. It was one of the humblest settlements in the capital of Akuahgrandia, very similar to Mae-uhkel's and his family's, and so was most of the crowd that thía. They looked simple but very happy and generally with very kind eyes... Suddenly, there was a tumultuous roar; people shouted and got excited. "Here comes Kelia!!!" Mae-uhkel heard, and as he turned around, he was struck by a wave of emotion from a roaring crowd that made his body tingle and awakened his vision. The glow in the chest of the candidate, who he saw from afar, was impressive. Additionally, she was literally – escorted– at an invisible level by beautiful heralds with shields of Light. Zaver radiated immense spirals of magenta light that reached directly to all the attendees and returned to her multiplied, and she seemed protected by an impenetrable blue sphere.

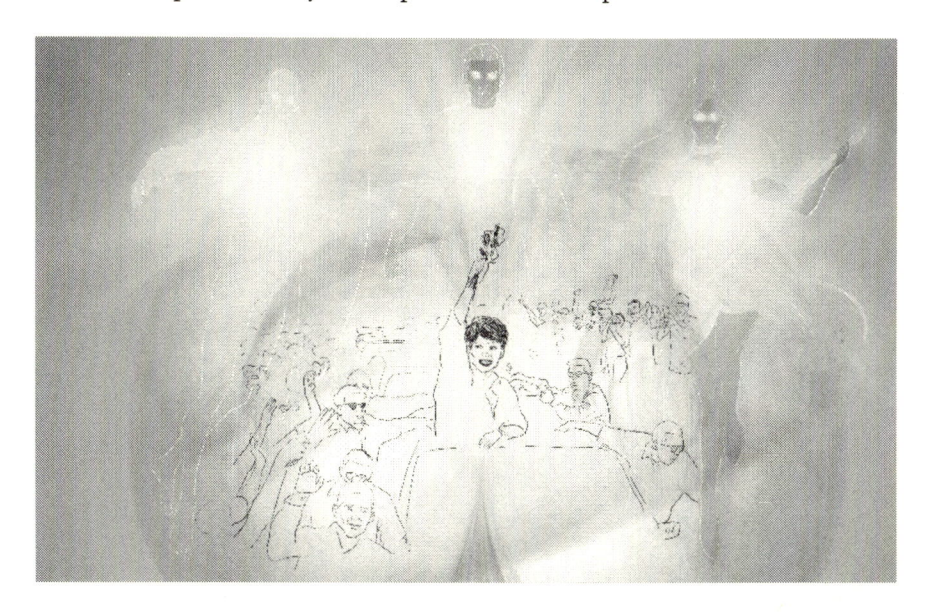

*https://opensea.io/collection/another-world-the-book*

    Mae-uhkel was surprised. But how was it possible that someone like this was up against Pawqar, it made no sense… or could it be… Kelia Zaver was Pawqar?! He looked for a small corner among the crowd to withdraw, breathe, and consult with his heart, hearing after a few seconds the clear voice of his guide who responded: "There is no gender where the true Self belongs, a being can incarnate as what is required. Remember, Gender exists everywhere; everything has its masculine and feminine principle. Pawqar must educate this world in Equity, Fraternity, and Freedom, virtues that are not exclusive to any gender and have rather been relegated by the huno's dominance in Hunum society. The leadership of a huna will bring balance."

    Indeed, Kelia Zaver, an independent candidate for **highest political role of Akuahgrandia**, was a Nomocat of the Great Council. A mature huna of mixed race, a resource administrator by training, a great hunumanist, with an intelligent gaze and the demeanor of a great diplomat. She had dedicated her life and career to what she described as 'a new way of doing real politics'. She was labeled a 'huna's defender', a term she herself rejected, due to her historical fight for the rights of the oppressed, hunas among them. What she truly defended were the basic principles of Equity, Freedom, and Fraternity. Perhaps because she was a huna, she firmly believed in Love as the universal source of positive change and practiced it in her actions. Her independent candidacy was due to her skepticism about the party structure; in fact, she joked about the word 'part-ies', implying the concept of division. A passionate lover of her country's history and the message of its liberators, she was, as her political opponents pejoratively called her, an – idealist. – Her mere candidacy was a challenge to the conservative view that a huna should never reach the Magnhunisy, under the empty argument that "no one in the world would respect us having a huna as 'Magnhuno'", which obviously belittled Zaver's capabilities. In short, she was truly an integral politician, and a real nuisance for the representatives of the established powers, which was why they kept her isolated from the main media.

The society of Akuahgrandia, like that of all Hunum, was led by people and entities full of corruption, anti-values, greed, and even class and racial hatred. They were busy keeping the masses asleep and manipulated through ignorance and fear. After the meeting in the Tres Raíces Street neighborhood, Kelia spoke with her campaign supervisor: "Nomocat, another victory today… we're now five points higher than last quint in the polls, but still far from Ragner. It's hard for us to get into the conventional media and reach the majority. Social networks have a limited reach to middle and upper-class sectors, but not to the less fortunate, who are the majority in our country. Most of those who support Ragner, especially from the middle and needier classes, do so only because he is the official party candidate. They have no way to contrast, compare. They don't know what we offer, they don't know us and haven't directly heard our proposal for change yet."

"Yes, you're right in what you say, Mara. however, we've been doing our real work with the people, in their communities, on the streets. Did you see today? Those people need us there with them… not in the media. It's true that spreading our message is important and we must spare no effort in that, but creating awareness and helping people organize themselves to solve their problems is the main thing and that's where most of the energies of our team should be focused."

"That's exactly what I'm telling you, Nomocat, the more people know us, I assure you, the more support we'll have, and we'll be able to help more. The best way to spread our ideas is through public and mass media. GlobaNet only reaches a very small sector."

"Yes, Mara, but understand that our message is not convenient for these media companies you want to convince. They are companies serving someone, either a person or a State; that's why the message they spread is what they want people to hear and, in our case, they don't want them to hear us. They are the ones selling the daily war against Deilgohu, under the pretext of being a terrorist country, but they don't say that the ruling elites of Z-suní and their allies here and around the world have economic and energy interests there, that they are the ones pulling the strings behind the terrorism they claim to fight. They're the ones that sell you an unsustainable lifestyle for the planet. Imagine if the media in the world were really used to bring education and healthy entertainment to people... growth! But no, they are businesses, and in business, there is no morality, only profits, and what brings more of it and more power is broadcasted. Lies, immorality, frivolity, and violence, because that controls, convinces, and 'sells'. They know that if we win the elections, they will be compelled by the demand of the people themselves to change their behavior and start working, not for more profits or more power, but to help improve people's life, but that's not 'profitable', Mara."

"But... I know very good people inside the media, Nomocat."

"And of course, there are many, but they are not the ones in charge. All of them obey 'editorial lines', which, do you know what they are?" she didn't wait for an answer "A group of people in high managerial positions who are in charge of separating the news from the crap and then they publish the crap."

"But there has to be a way, Nomocat Zaver…"

"By Gaemo I wish, Mara, I wish!"

Mae-uhkel, for his part, rushed to the channel after the rally, hurriedly looking for Nissa to tell her about his discovery when he bumped into Galek, who stopped him in his tracks.

*https://opensea.io/collection/another-world-the-book*

"Hey, hey, where are we rushing off to?" Realizing it was Galek, Mae-uhkel was happy to see him and energized the virtue of Elevation in white color in him to say: "How are you, Galar Zoren-Zic? I'm very excited because I've just seen candidate Kelia Zaver. Do you know her?"

"I do not, really—at least not personally—but she seems like an interesting person and certainly profound in what she proposes," Galek responded.

Mae-uhkel was pleased with Galek's response, since, as a representative of the ruling elite, his perception could have been different. But it did not surprise him too much, knowing who he was dealing with.

"I have been with her. Her proposal is honest and serious, Galar. I tell you, as a huno, I would be proud to be governed by a huna like her. But most of the information about her is very biased and pejorative. We should interview her, Galar Galek, here on the channel," said Mae-uhkel, in an attempt to reinforce Galek's ideas and pave the way for Pawqar.

"I don't know, I don't think it fits our line," Galek said, avoiding going into details and expressing his ideas, which he knew were different.

"Please think about it... well, I'll leave you as I'm in a hurry, but do you think you could grant me an appointment later, Galar? I would like to talk to you about something," he said, seeking to close the distance between them and thus awaken him to his mission.

"Yes, I noticed you're in a hurry. Sure, come by my office and tell the assistant."

"Thank you very much, Galar."

Mae-uhkel continued his quest for Nissa and upon finding her, he said excitedly, "Nissa, you were right, Kelia Zaver is wonderful,"

"Ha, ha, ha, aaah, and how did you change your mind so quickly?" his friend asked.

Mae-uhkel knew he couldn't tell her the truth, so he quickly made up a story.

I went to her campaign headquarters, investigated more deeply about her as you recommended, and we went to the neighborhoods and the villages, with the people... It's true what her slogan says, she really believes in Love as a source of change, and in Equity, Freedom, and Fraternity as the main virtues of a governing system." Then he seemed to ponder something and said, "Nissa, we have to get her some space here on the channel..."

"You know what, that sounds like a very good idea indeed but…" she hesitated "I see it as very difficult, Mae- uhkel. I don't think the channel would benefit from spreading her message... besides, I'm still very new here and no one would listen to me," she added at the end.

"But it's important, Nissa, you know that more than anyone. We must find a way," said Mae- uhkel, energizing Elevation, Will, and Wisdom in his friend. "We have to make sure people hear her. Her hunumanity, her message, and her intentions are unknown to most, and the channel has a lot of reach, Nissa. Come on, you must know someone to talk to."

Meditating for a moment, she then said: "You know, in fact, I do know someone. I'll think about it, okay?"

That evening, Mae-uhkel did his Connection Exercise, remembering the first Law, 'The ALL is MIND; the universe is mental. EVERYTHING occurs first in the mind.' He then used his mind to visualize Zaver delivering her message to all the Akuahgrandians through the channel, sending energy of will to Nissa so that she could find within herself the strength and the way to achieve it.

The next thía, Nissa woke up with the idea in her head and called Galek: "Good morning, love, how did you sleep? Listen, I need to talk to you about something, are you going to the plant today?"

"Sure, see you there…"

"No, let's meet at Lombardo instead."

"Okay, I'm leaving right away!"

At the Shazaá, Nissa asked him:

"So, you want me to propel changes in this channel, right? well… what do you think about the idea of interviewing Kelia Zaver?" Galek immediately remembered the conversation with Mae-uhkel, which had pleased him, and he replied:

"You're not the first person to tell me this recently, I love it, but it's very difficult, love, you know how things are here and I don't have the power to decide on that."

"I know, but I mean we could devise a strategy," she said thoughtfully.

Suddenly, an idea occurred to Galek. "Unless… what we want is to ridicule the 'huna's defender, idealist, and resentful one.'"

"Are you serious?" said Nissa, "what are you saying? Have you gone crazy?"

"Of course, listen, that's how we're going to sell it to the executives, in fact, not an interview, but a debate, nationally televised, imagine the ratings: 'THE DEBATE OF THE CYCLE' and our argument is that it will be the final blow to the populist… Since Ragner is so well-prepared, he will surely 'make her look ridiculous live, coast to coast.'"

"You're a genius!!!" She hugged him before kissing him

"Ha, ha, ha, let me see what I can do"

Meanwhile, Etzuko had been contacting her friends in the government. The most interested was Nomocat Zaver, who, upon hearing about an investigation of an ecological and alternative energy source, became very enthusiastic and asked Etzuko for a meeting to present the project and see how it could be supported.

Thus, it happened, in the subsequent quints, Zaver convened several Akauhgrandian scientists and energy experts who were friends. Although they warned her of the delicacy of the subject, Kelia felt that she should give it a chance, given the scientist's credentials, and the word spread quickly in the small academic environment. They met at the National Major School of Akuahgrandia where some of them were titular boeharas. Upon arriving, Masaru's daughter Etzuko introduced him to Nomocat Zaver, the architect of the meeting, and she did the same for him to the rest of the panel.

*https://opensea.io/collection/another-world-the-book*

Immediately, Masaru thanked them for the interest shown in inviting him to present his work and, with his characteristic passion, briefly and informally explained the origin of his research and the motivations he had. To Nomocat Zaver, the speech seemed familiar, but she couldn't quite remember where she had heard it. In the rush of her busy life, her travel on the plane that brought Munai to Akuahgrandian lands and Masaru's conversation with an elderly huna about the complex Eco Synthesis were long forgotten, at least to her conscious memory. "Shall we move on to the presentation?" Masaru proposed, and so they did, starting a discussion that lasted for hours: "We can then achieve energy liberation through an induced electrochemical reaction. I have been using a Nictadium rod as a key ingredient. This metal is abundant in nature, which makes it very low-cost. Moreover, I have recorded an incredibly high capacity for absorbing immense amounts of dimenium, almost one hundred thousand times its volume. Then what we do is use 'heavy ákuah' — replacing the trisfacio essential particles with dimenium— and a simple electrolytic cell, with one pole of a common metal like Saliciato and an opposite pole of Nictadium..."

"One moment, one moment, Munai," interrupted one of the attendees. "Is it just me, or does this sound very similar to the 'experiment' of the 'infamously famous' Ponsmann and Fleisch?"

"Thank you for your question. I'll give you the short version to conclude the presentation, and we can delve deeper in private afterward if you wish. Certainly, the 'achievement,' as I would call it, of Ponsmann and Fleisch served as both inspiration and a basis for our studies. First, we corroborated what they observed, which is quite significant, as it contradicts the reports produced at that time. However, we have our own theory regarding it." After saying this, Masaru explained the process in enough detail that even the skeptical scientists began to wonder if he might have actually succeeded, prompting them to ask more inquisitive questions. Hmmm, do you have control over all the variables? Have you achieved results that are sufficiently controlled, predictable, stable, and repeatable? Because that was the main 'challenge' in the fiasco cycles ago!"

"Well, I don't like the word 'fiasco,' since their work has been very useful for us as a starting point. And yes, you are right, that question has several facets. So far, the results are random, unpredictable, and unstable, but the experiment is repeatable. That is, there is always a reaction, which is why we continue working. At first, we believed that the main reason for the instability, for example, was the hygroscopy of the heavy ákuah; that, in its exposure to the atmosphere, quickly replaced the dimenium with the trisfacios found in the air and left the material inert. But we performed the experiment in a vacuum obtaining similar results. Part of what remains for us to do is to introduce another variant to consider and that is to have control at the essential level of the structure of the metal, something that was impossible back in the cycles when Ponsmann and Fleisch, and thus control and predict the location of the cracks. Thanks to today's technology, we have enough control at essential level, which would allow us; for example, to create simple cubes with nanoscopic grids in layers of Nictadium of infinitesimal thickness, let's say a couple of essential particles thick, sandwiched with a permeable material slightly thicker than the essential particle of ákuah, to allow its passage. This would generate a volume of multiple films, which would be the reactive spaces, separated from each other, to have multiple reactions at the same time. If it works, I calculate, with a piece of this size, – he said using his index and thumb fingers, opened to mid- range, – it would generate enough energy to supply a household for a lifetime. Of course, to develop these and other ideas that arise, equipment and financial support are needed and that is what we request from you today... Thank you very much! –

Finally, Masaru left most of the panel members amazed, including Nomocat Zaver herself, as she approached one of the attending experts to talk to him, she was already beginning to imagine even greater possibilities in her head and think of ways to help Munai Takashi continue with his research.

However, on the other hand, one of the attendees, a boehara from the Major School, discreetly left the group and made a call:

*https://opensea.io/collection/another-world-the-book*

"Yes? Sekk? It's me, I have some very important news that I think you'll be interested in, let's meet urgently this dahna and I'll tell you."

Meanwhile, the individual who had chatted with Nomocat Zaver approached Masaru: "Munai?" he shook his hand. "First of all, thank you very much for such a brilliant presentation and for sharing your advances with us. We are amazed, you have made us all dream here," he said with a smile. "I am Munai Domaar, director of the school of Applied Psychophysics and Senior Director of the Nuclear Physics and Alternative Energies area. Nomocat Zaver was kind enough to tell me about your work and invite me. She has been a great friend and collaborator of our institution for cycles, and to tell the truth, a great enthusiast of education in general, advances, and all those things. I was quite impressed with your work and would be honored to have someone of your caliber on our team of boeharas and researchers. I would like you to consider the possibility of occupying a chair at our Major School. If you are interested, we would offer you all the support within our possibilities, our facilities with access to the technology you mentioned, and your own laboratory. The Major School has funding for research projects, and we would be honored if yours were one of them. But please, don't feel pressured in any way to answer me now, enjoy your dahna. Here is my card. Think about it and give me a call later if you're interested.

Excitedly he answered: "Oh, thank you very much, Munai. Sure, I'll call you."

Etzuko was at his side and witnessed all of Munai Domaar's compliments and his offer. As soon as Munai Doomar left, she jumped on her father in a euphoric hug. "Did you see, dad? Now we'll be together here in Akuahgrandia, you and I, and you can continue with your work. No more separation between us, everything that happens, happens for a greater good."

"Yes, daughter, yes. You have always said that…"

They hugged each other and celebrated what promised to be a new beginning for someone who had devoted his life to what he truly felt was achievable, a cheap and clean energy source, which would grant a better future to his sick planet.

*https://opensea.io/collection/another-world-the-book*

However, hours later, at the house of candidate Ragner, a meeting took place between him and the boehara attendee of Takashi's presentation:

"Yes, Kelia Zaver was the organizer of the meeting and Munai's studies seem well underway, though he doesn't seem to be very sure of the definitive solution yet." Ragner remained thoughtful for a while, then asked: "Do you think he'll really achieve it?"

"It seems he has made interesting discoveries, and what he proposes is simple but logical. In fact, he seems to have had some small results; the has dedicated his whole life to the subject and is one of the world's leading authorities. He is one of the few in the world who has dared to resume the studies of Ponsmann and Fleisch. It wouldn't be strange that, if there is a missing piece, he will be who find it... of course if the support he's asking for given. That is why I think, if you get involved in this, it could help a lot in your campaign, can you imagine what your image would be like if you appeared as the financier of something like this? Besides the unimaginable economic gain of that patent, you would be the owner of the most powerful energy source on the planet! Don't let Zaver be the one to do it. Get ahead of her Sekk and support the huno."

"Yes, it could be... Keep a close eye on his progress and keep me updated, we'll see."

After concluding the meeting, Ragner picked up the nokó: "Ambassador? Good evening, Sekk Ragner here. I have information that might be of interest."

---

Galek brings the idea of the debate to the channel's board. His proposal was strategic—he intended to place Nissa as the host, knowing that her balanced approach could give Kelia Zaver's message a fair platform. The board loved the idea and accepted, however, while appreciating the concept, decided to assign the role to Kkraso Ehf instead. Kkraso was known for his strong alignment with Ragner's conservative views and a fierce opponent of Kelia's ideas, ensuring the debate will be anything but neutral. A few thías later, Mara arrived with an envelope in hand at Nomocat Zaver's office: "Candidate, we did it! Look." The envelope contained a letter that read:

*'Invitation: Nomocat Kelia Zaver, Independent Candidate for the Magnhunist of the Republic of Akuahgrandia,*

*TUUS World Network is pleased to invite you to a debate to be held in our Main Studio facilities, live, in prime time, between you and the candidate of the VdP party, Sekk Ragner. The moderator will be Galar Kkraso Ehf.*

*Please confirm your participation.'*

Mara and Zaver embraced. "Well, I think we got it Mara!" exclaimed Zaver with envelope still in her hand.

"Yes, galera, yes...and the best thing is that the rest the media, all of them, of all kinds will connect to the signal. Everybody is going to hear us!!!"

"Very well, then we must be prepared," said Zaver. "Mara, confirm our participation right away. Everyone else, let's prepare the material for the debate. Forward, team! We are on the right track!" –

The next thía, the eyes of all Akuahgrandia were on the screens, with the political meeting between the two main candidates.

The strategy was to exalt Ragner by pitting him against an easily defeatable contender like Zaver. The candidate of the ruling party represented continuity. Although he was with old politics, he spoke of change, of attracting foreign investments, and of preserving the – achievements – they had so far. It was an empty and somewhat trite discourse, but still had great support due to the fear to the unknown, of the real change represented by Zaver.

For her part, Kelia represented a breath of fresh air, exuding independence and pioneering ideas.

She championed change too, but grounded her visions in the principles of Universal Love and Philosophy as means to feel and understand the needs of the people. She stood firm in defending the ideas of the liberators of Akuahgrandia. Her proposals included offering care to the most vulnerable, restructuring education to be free and more focused on uplifting hunumanity, and promoting health maintenance and protection with universal, free access for all—a paradigm shift aimed at enhance the capability of individuals to contribute to society as well as their quality of life. Everybody working for all. She advocated for equal opportunities without discrimination and for stimulating national capital in cooperation with state efforts to forge a better society. For all these reasons, she was seen by the more conservative sectors as a threat, and the smear campaign against her was savage.

The moderator's preference for candidate Ragner was evident, of course. His victory was a guarantee of maintaining the status of the station. The wealthy Zoren Zic owned an entire network of audio and RB stations, as well as Globanet and print media, which gave him almost a communicational monopoly in the country. He achieved this thanks to a macabre mutualism with the governments of Akuahgrandia who had granted him all the concessions in exchange for using them to shape public opinion in favor of their interests. Zaver, within her proposal for change, proposed to democratize communication spaces, and that of course, meant reviewing all the concessions, which was unacceptable for Zoren Zic and his partners. It would mean the beginning of the end of the media empire. In short, the debate seemed became more like a trap than an opportunity for Zaver.

*https://opensea.io/collection/another-world-the-book*

The debate was heavily biased, just as planned. The moderator, favoring Ragner, posed tricky, tendentious questions, leaving little room for Kelia to provide complete answers. He was determined to undermine Zaver's credibility and reinforce the status quo. His partiality was unmistakable, and he used all his experience to ensure that the interests of the wealthy media mogul Zoren Zic—and those of the ruling powers—remained unchallenged. At the end of the debate, he urged Zaver, to say a few last words. Referring to her pejoratively as "the idealist," he made sure to call her that repeatedly during the entire debate, concluding with, "Let's then give the floor, for a final message, to the opposition idealist candidate, Kelia Zaver."

"Thank you, Galar Ehf. I feel very nervous being here, in front of all of you who I think expect us to have answers to your problems and those of our society. Well, first of all, I want to make it clear that my candidacy is independent. And it is independent not because of arrogance, sectarianism, or egotism. It is simply independent because I, along with and the hunas and hunos who support me and have been traveling this path together for several cycles, think that the solution is certainly not what we have today, but also—and in this I want to be emphatic so that you, hear me, Galar Presenter— I want to add that the solution is not either in the camp that opposes it. For decades, we have been pulling the country, some to one side, others to the opposite side, and what we are really getting that way is tearing it in half. Some ideologies demand Freedom, others Fraternity and Equity. Are any of them wrong? Aren't all these virtues equally necessary and deserving of coexistence in balance to achieve an integral society? The time has come for us, all of us, to abandon our old paradigms of separatism and together, hear me well, NOT Kelia Zaver and her followers but ALL TOGETHER, push Akuahgrandia, not to one side, not to the other, but upward, which is where we all really want to go. Brother Ragner to you and all your team and followers is also the call, because we are all necessary and we have ideas, virtues, and talents to contribute. Let us abandon competition, punishment, and even reward which have done so much harm to us as hunumanity, and encourage cooperation, empathy, and acknowledgment of each other. Education, understanding our needs and those of others. After all, we all want the same thing, an Akuahgrandia with peace, security, prosperity, brotherhood... a better Akuahgrandia, a better Hunum. Let's be capable of creating a new path, to a new country that sets the example of a new world. – *Another World* where Universal Love is the main goal, because no system can be sustained in time if it is not based on Love, understanding, and compassion. Let's give equal opportunity to everyone and to each according to what they contribute to their fellow beings, to the society they inhabit. Let's encourage solidarity, that is the fairest, freest, and most egalitarian system. Because Love is wise and at the same time is just. The Will in the cultivation of that Love and that Wisdom will lead us to understand and accept more and more, every thía, our Equality hence we can Equity to our society. Only then will we be truly capable of analyzing our differences. If we want change, we must start by changing ourselves. Let's not be satisfied with who we are. We can all grow. We all can love more, accept more, hear more and support more. Let's dare to change, let's dare to believe and to create. If we are capable of believing, we will be capable of seeing, not the other way around. Beloved Akuagrandeans, I am here to serve you. My only ambition is for Akuahgrandia to occupy the place it deserves. I am not a chosen one, I am just another hunuman, like all of you, who calls you to build, together, the Homeland we dream of the new Homeland. Together we can make our Homeland Another World, a New World where Love, Equity, and Peace reign. All my love to you, my brothers and sisters, children of Akuahgrandia, children of Hunum. –

At the end of Zaver's speech, the entire audience, moved, cheered for her. Even the Kkraso gave a euphoric applause as if carried by an uncontrollable impulse that he then repressed upon realizing what he was doing. Ragner scowled, furious that the strategy to ridicule Zaver in front of the country had failed and, on the contrary, had provided the platform that Zaver's message had been needing.

---

Late into the dahna, Mae-uhkel's nokó rang. He turned over in bed and clumsily answered the call, still half asleep:

"Hello?"

"Mae-uhkel? Were you sleeping? I'm sorry, but I've just come from meeting with a friend in the International Department and I have information that might be very useful to you, but if you prefer, we can talk as soon as Thía breaks…"

"No Nissa, please," Mae-uhkel interrupted her. "I appreciate it so much, I'm very interested, tell me, what you got?"

"No, but I think it's too long to talk about here and I also have things to show you. Can we meet at Lombardo? Does that work for you?" – –

"Sure, fine…" he said while rushing out of the bed "…but you might have to wait for me a bit… It's hard to get out of my house by collective transport this late."

"I understand, don't worry, see you there."

"Alright, see you in a bit"

Later at Shazaá Lombardo, Nissa was waiting for Mae-uhkel seated at the bar:

"A Hoojani, double, please," Nissa ordered her spirit cocktail from the bartender when Mae-uhkel arrived, they moved to a table and when seated she said:

"Well, I've found out some things. Regarding Eco Synthesis energy, it seems so good that it's considered by most to be a fantasy. If achieved, it would really change the course of history. Also, if we look at the facts with a bit more suspicion than usual, it seems there is someone or something behind, hindering advances wherever they arise. Indeed, as you said, the most significant advances are attributed to a group from the National Major School of Lukón in Shunsuke." The waiter brought her drink, she took a sip and continued. "They were working until a few Conjunctions ago, and here's the bad news: the project was closed without further explanation."

"Do you know who was in charge of the team? What happened to that person?"

"Yes, it was…" she said sorting some papers from her folder "…Munai Masaru Takashi," she said, showing him a photograph. "But nothing is known about him; at the Major School, there are rumors that after the Project's cancellation, he left the country of Lukón but nobody knows for sure."

"He's here in Akuahgrandia!" Mae-uhkel exclaimed, remembering the plan and the session at the Great Council. However, for Nissa, it was so unthinkable that she took it as a joke.

"Yes, can you imagine?" she said with a mocking smile, finishing her drink. Her mental field became vulnerable cause the effect of the drink, which allowed one of the Tumsas stalking her to sneak an idea into her head: "Turn off the nokó, so you're not interrupted."

*https://opensea.io/collection/another-world-the-book*

She did so and continued the conversation:

"No, I'm serious! Look, Nissa," Mae-uhkel took Nissa's hands, looked into her eyes, and putting all the intension in his words he said, "Please don't ask me how I know, but trust me, I know that boehara Takashi is here in Akuahgrandia. Could you find out for me, Nissa, please?"

Just as their hands were still held by Mae-uhkel, Galek, who happened to be passing by, saw the scene from outside the Shazaá and recognized Mae-uhkel, whom he knew from the channel.

https://opensea.io/collection/another-world-the-book

Confused, he hid and quickly left, intending not to be seen. Barhana's venomous words resonated in the young huno's head once more, but now with more force, sowing doubt and leading him to misinterpret the situation.

The conversation continued at the Shazaá: "Well, I guess so, but I don't understand anything."

"I need to find out the whereabouts of boehara Takashi, if he's here in Akuahgrandia, I must meet with him as soon as possible." Mae-uhkel's eagerness in explaining the situation to his friend grew with every word.

"Mae-uhkel, you're scaring me, this seems to go beyond a thesis."

"Yes, Nissa, let me see if I can explain a bit. Remember what I told you happened. The story is more disturbing than you can imagine. Twenty-five cycles ago, two chemists from Khermeno, Ponsmann and Fleisch, claimed to have succeeded, but they made several mistakes in the way they publish their results. The first mistake was not communicating it through the 'sacred book' of Science in Hunum, the Nuestro Mundo journal, but instead, they called a press conference with the main media of the time. Moreover, it was a sudden and unexpected blow both for Sápea companies and for the entire large energy industry, which had spent billions on the development of dangerous and polluting hot synthesis reactors. A device that fit on a desk and was super cheap was going to produce a thousand times more energy than their complicated and huge nuclear plants. But what ultimately finished them off was publishing before achieving stable results. They expected to get funding, but naively didn't count on the dominant power. The government of Z-Suní funded the Major School of Jotmá to 'reproduce' the results and 'validate' the chemists' experiment…"

"Of course," said Nissa ironically.

"Then, at the end of the study, they said in their report that it was impossible and even worse, that it was absurd to obtain what Ponsmann and Fleisch claimed. This was enough to bury the careers of the chemists and their experiment. Nobody ever talked about Eco Synthesis again, and even in Z-Suní, based on the report from the Major School of Jotmá, they banned the registration of any patent related to the subject. These two scientists disappeared from the map after their funding was withdrawn… Currently, there are few people working in the area despite it possibly being an incredible energy solution."

"It sounds like a whole conspiracy…"

"Yes, and you haven't heard this… Over the cycles, they discovered that the scientists from the Major School of Jotmá had altered their results to discredit Ponsmann and Fleisch.

"No way! And that was just left like that?"

"Almost. There was an internal uproar in the Major School, resignations of some involved, but externally only a small amendment to the original report was made, scrupulously written, of course, where they recognized 'small inaccuracies in the enthalpy analysis.' They also changed their evaluation of their results: from an irrefutable 'unable to reproduce Ponsmann and Fleisch's experiment' to a lukewarm 'excessively inconclusive and erratic to be confirmed.'

"What a scandal…!!!" exclaimed Nissa.

"Yes, so, obviously, you're aware of the delicate situation between Z-suní and Deilgohu, right? "Yes, of course, but what does that have to do with it?" asked the young huna, visibly confused. "Wait." Mae-uhkel decided to touch the combative and rebellious fiber of the informatist, as he couldn't reveal who he really was. "Think it again, if you review Z-suní's military actions over the last cycles, you'll see that…"

"They are all somehow related to Energy," said the informatist, well versed in world geopolitics. "Of course! Particularly Sápea." She continued her analysis "The main families holding power in that country, including the Zoren Zics, are all major shareholders or money guards financing Sápea companies, arms manufacturers, BRs, and/or main construction companies, which get the contracts for resource exploitation and reconstruction of the invaded and destroyed cities. Besides, the Sápea reserves in Z-suní are about to run out. They haven't found new conventional deposits for decades, and those that remain are almost depleted. Therefore, they need a new supplier or to continue exploiting unconventional deposits that are polluting, expensive, and dangerous.

"Exactly, and that would take away the monopoly and power from the Sápea companies…"

"Yes, and their Sápea-currency would collapse… plus, with such a cheap and inexhaustible energy source available to all countries, it would mean the end of Z-suní's hegemony…Oh great Gaemo"

"Exactly, right, does it all make sense? so they are people financed by that government to prevent the emergence of Eco Synthesis."

"This is more delicate than I imagined."

"Are you scared?" asked Mae-uhkel.

"No… I love it! But what's your interest in all this? Why get involved and risk something like this?"

"Well, it started as a college project but while I went deeper became in actions for… I don't know, for the love of science and maybe because I'm an idealist…"

"That's what people usually call me," they both laughed.

"But, besides assumptions and speculations, do you have any proof?"

"Not really, no, that's why I'd like to talk to boehara Takashi, I want to know what happened to his research and how far he could go. I'm sure he's in Akuahgrandia."

"But that's totally absurd, Mae-uhkel. Why would that Munai expert in Eco Synthesis be here in Akuahgrandia? He could be anywhere in the world, even the rumors might not be true and he's still in Lukón working for a private party, perhaps."

"Nissa," Mae-uhkel told her, looking into her eyes and focusing on her heart, radiating a green and white light that enveloped Nissa in order for her to be elevated and able to see the Truth in his words, "I know that Munai is here, trust me and I swear I won't let you down, if you want to get to the bottom of this, help me and I guarantee you the best story of your career."

Without knowing why, Nissa felt a great trust in Mae-uhkel's words and from that moment decided to team up with the young student.

While this was happening at Shazaá Lombardo, Galek was driving his vehicle aimlessly. His pride hurt and the ghost of jealousy enveloping him, he drove for hours. He took his nokó, dialed Nissa's code to ask for an explanation. Of course, she has it turned off... With Barhana's words repeating over and over in his head; he decided to call her, after all, she was the only common contact with Nissa:

"Hello Barhi, good evening!" Barhana noticed the broken tone in Galek's voice and asked: "Hello, friend, is something wrong? Is everything okay with your dad?"

"Yes, yes, well he's the same, hey, by any chance, do you have another nokóde for Nissa?" It was easy for Barhana to guess that something was going on between them, so she didn't miss the opportunity to sow discord again.

"Not really, remember she's not my friend Galek. And, by the way, why are you looking for another nokóde for her... don't tell me she's already done one of her things to you and that I was right?

"No, actually it's because I've been calling the one, I have and I can't get through, but it's very strange."

"Very strange? She must be up to something that she doesn't want you to talk to her..." Immediately Galek had the image of Nissa with Mae-uhkel holding hands and felt a void in his stomach, but he didn't let Barhana know.

"I don't think so, well, friend, thank you then," As he ended the call, his pain didn't allow him to reason. Instead of waiting and talk to Nissa to clarify the situation, urged on by Barhana's venomous words, he speculated and created a whole story of lies and infidelity in his head. It seemed that the dark forces were doing their job and enveloping one of those called to fight them, attacking him at his weakest point, pride. These low feelings allowed room in Galek's life for the energies projected by the shadows who knew who he was and therefore attacked him more fiercely. He needed to get out of that emotional state quickly or else he would be an easy target for the side of the shadows.

# CHAPTER VII

## THE SECRET IS IN THE ÁKUAH

The next thía, after seeing Galek's call log from the previous dahna, Nissa tried to call him insistently but without success. She left several worried messages. Then she went to his office as soon as she arrived at the channel and waited for him there. Upon his arrival, she saw that he was at least okay; he came accompanied by some coworkers and discussing channel matters. She interrupted them: "Hello, good morning, Galek, can we talk?"

"Sorry, but as you can see, I'm a bit busy right now," he replied somewhat coldly.

"Will you have a moment later to talk to me?" she asked formally, under the watchful eyes of all those accompanying him.

"Yes, I'll let you know by nokó message."

Nissa noticed his cold and evasive attitude and couldn't understand why. He didn't send any messages or contact her in any way during the thía. She decided to wait for him that evening as he left the channel. There she questioned him:

"Hello Galek, you didn't respond to my messages."

"I was very busy all thía, I called you many times last dahna and strangely your nokó was off, where were you?"

"Working." Nissa didn't want to give him details of her work with

Mae-uhkel due to the sensitivity of the topic and out of respect for the young huno's initial request. But this was mistakenly interpreted by Galek, who felt deceived. "Oh, okay, well, anything else you want to tell me?"

"But, what's wrong, love? What's happening? Let's talk, what's bothering you?" she said as she approached him intending to embrace and kiss him, but he rejected her.

"Nothing, you know, I'm in a hurry now, we'll talk later," he said, removing her hands and continuing towards his vehicle.

"Galek, wait! Galek!!!" The young huno didn't respond, getting into his vehicle and driving off. Nissa was deeply hurt by Galek's treatment, which she didn't believe she deserved, and also very confused about the reasons for his behavior.

In the following thías, Mae-uhkel resumed his duties, though most of his attention was on the task he had to fulfill. He saw Galek enter the channel but was surprised to see a Tumsa near him, seeming to instill various dark thoughts and ideas into the troubled young huno's mental field. He also saw two very small Bham-yis following him, one he could clearly identify as that of cigarettes, but he didn't recognize the other. He tried to cross paths with Galek to greet him, but Galek seemed elusive and hurried, not even exchanging greetings. Mae-uhkel tried to help, using his heart's power, but the energy of his attempts remained floating a few centimeters around without being able to penetrate his mental field, unable to reach him... then he heard Leyhana's voice... – He is now very internally unbalanced, closed off to receiving any help you want to give him. – Mae-uhkel then tried to read what was going on in his friend's mind but couldn't either. – That goes against his free will. His problems are his own and only he decides with whom he shares them, – Leyhana indicated again.

*https://opensea.io/collection/another-world-the-book*

That afternoon, Nissa decided to look for Galek again in his office, but to no avail. He wasn't there. She asked his assistant, who indicated she had no information. A bit upset by the young huno's inexplicable attitude, she headed back to her office while also speculating about the whereabouts of Munai Takashi. She had tried all the channel contacts and correspondents in Lukón, but nothing. None of the rest of the Major Schools and Institutes that could potentially be advancing such experiments had any information either. Even the Oriental Nation's Ministry of Science had no information. Almost giving up, Nissa thought again about Mae-uhkel's idea, although she had already dismissed it because, even if he were in Akuahgrandia, she wouldn't know where to begin her search. She thought for a moment, served herself a Shazaá, and while walking back and forth in the copying and printing room, trying to think of an idea, the Shazaá spilled over the table, onto an old nokóde guide. Nissa took some napkins from her drawer to clean the spilled Shazaá and at that moment, it occurred to her. She could search the guide, of course, if he really was in the country, it would be simple because how many Takashis could there be in Akuahgrandia? She rushed to her office and searched, finding five, but no Masaru. Slightly disappointed, she noted the five numbers and picked up the nokó. After three attempts: a restaurant, a spare parts store, and a galera who didn't speak very good Akuahgrandean, none knew any Masaru. The fourth time a voicemail answered: "Hello, this is Etzuko, please leave your message after the beep." Nissa thought about leaving a message but immediately considered it a bad idea and hung up the call to try the last nokóde without success. She sighed in frustration and then exclaimed, "Gaemo, what do I do?" Then an idea came to her mind. Using her informatist's card, she could go to the embassy; after all, perhaps they would have a record of lukoneses residing in Akuahgrandia. She took her bag and left the building heading to the consular office. Upon arrival, she was received at the reception and referred to the director of immigration, who provided her with a list, whichthey began to review together. Meanwhile, Etzuko was working in her office when one of her Gaemas guides projected an idea into her mind: "You've been working for a long time, go out and get some fresh air." She stopped what she was doing, sighed deeply, and did so. Meanwhile, Nissa found nothing and the director kindly accompanied her to the exit. There, disheartened, she thanked the official: "Thank you very much anyway, Galar Kabuto, here's my card, if you hear of any Masaru Takashi, please let me know, with the person's consent, of course. "At that moment, coincidentally, Etzuko passed through the reception on her way to her break and couldn't help but overhear the conversation. She approached, inferring that Nissa was someone from the Major School, and asked:

"Excuse me, I heard you're looking for Munai Takashi?

"Yes, the Physicochemist," replied an excited yet incredulous Nissa.

"Are you from the Major School?"

"No, not really, I'm an informatist and was looking for information about his research."

"Ah, I see. Nice to meet you," said the young huna, extending her hand to Nissa. "My name is Etzuko, Etzuko Takashi, and Munai Takashi is my father."

Nissa couldn't believe it. "The pleasure is mine, Galera Takashi. It's great to meet you. Your father is admirable. I'm currently doing a report on alternative energies and have thoroughly researched his advances in Lukón. Do you know how I could contact him and if he'd be open to granting me an interview for GlobaNet?"

"I'll ask him, but I think he'll agree. He loves talking about his stuff, but coincidentally, my dad is here in Akuahgrandia, he arrived a few quints ago."

Nissa paled, Mae-uhkel was right, but how? "Do you think I'll be able to contact him, Galera Takashi?"

"Yes, I don't think there will be a problem. I'll ask him and let you know."

"Fantastic, look, here's my card. Please tell him that if he agrees, we'll be contacting him soon for an interview, okay?"

"Sure..."

"Sorry, Nissa Berdat is my name, it's there on the card," she said, pointing to it.

"Alright Nissa, I'll give your message to my dad."

Nissa immediately left to call Mae-uhkel, took her nokó and dialed. It was common for him not to answer, so Nissa left him a voice message: "I don't know how the heck, but you were right, little wizard! Munai Masaru is in Akuahgrandia!!! But not only that... you'll love me because... You'll get your interview! I'll tell you more later. Yes, I know I'm wonderful."

---

On election thía in Akuahgrandia, despite the debate seeming to have had a profound effect on the electorate's perception, it was unclear what impact it had on Nomocat Zaver's popularity. At that point, she was second in the polls but far behind Ragner before the broadcast. The debate marked the official end of the campaigns, making it impossible for pollsters to gauge its effect. The people of Akuahgrandia poured into the streets to vote en masse. Unlike all previous elections, the abstention rate was extremely low, with eight out of ten Akuahgrandians casting their vote, legitimizing the process and demonstrating unusual political enthusiasm. However, after the long and crowded election contest ended, the state institutions, all in dark hands, began to slow down the vote counting and the delivery of results under various pretexts. "Due to data transmission problems and with fifty-five percent of the votes still uncounted, it is impossible for us to give a result at this time. Although the trend seems to favor candidate Ragner, no one should claim victory yet. The total results will be given in the following thías," announced the Electoral Tribunal.

Meanwhile, Galek, influenced by the dark forces, was deteriorating internally. During these thías, Galar Drakur Zoren Zic finally succumbed to his illness. After several thías, Galek decided to take charge of the channel, more to assert himself as the supreme supervisor and thereby influence Nissa, than because he really wanted the position. On the thía of his official appointment, a modest corporate reception was held, attended by all the informatists, editors, and the executive staff of the channel. Nissa attended and tried several times to approach Galek, whom she hadn't seen since his father's funeral, where he continued to distance himself from her. Surrounded by executives, he was eager to talk to Nissa, but his intoxicated state left him at the mercy of the dark forces. His wounded pride prevented him from listening to his heart, causing him to avoid her all evening. Tired of trying, Nissa left disappointed, and he stayed drowning his sorrows, in the company of those who were now – his executives, – which also became a frequent practice.

The next thía, Mae-uhkel's nokó rang; it was Nissa:

"Nissa, thank you..." Nissa interrupted him.

"Yes, Mae-uhkel, you can thank me in person, Munai Takashi can see us right now in his laboratory. Shall we go?"

"Ah, yes, great, of course!"

"Good, I'll pick you up at your place."

"Alright!"

Masaru's research continued in his laboratory at the Major School. He was about to test his idea of the sandwiched cube. With everything ready, he began injecting energy into the electrolytic cell. Moments later, an incipient golden-blue flame formed on the surface of the cube.

*https://opensea.io/collection/another-world-the-book*

Masaru's heart beat faster, a gentle smile spread across his face, but just before he began to celebrate, the flickering flame—produced by micro-explosions—extinguished after a few moments of burning. Masaru checked the sensors: Mega ray emission, a large number of free Halure essential particles... undoubtedly Eco Synthesis. The layered cube idea had worked. It was a step forward, but nothing stable or lasting. What was happening? It was as if he was missing some crucial factor. He erased and rewrote some notes on the board, then reported the results on his proccuan before sitting down, deep in thought about what had just transpired.

Outside the laboratory, Mae-uhkel and Nissa arrived for the interview. They approached the lab door, but before knocking, the young huno took the informatist's hand and said: "Nissa, no matter what I say in there, please trust me completely. You might hear me say things you don't understand, but believe me, I won't say more or less than necessary." Nissa nodded her head, though not understanding what Mae-uhkel meant. Before entering, the young seer projected and energized the golden wisdom and green truth energies directly into the hearts of Munai and his friend. Arriving, they saw the scientist through the top window of the laboratory door, seated and staring fixedly at the experimental setup. They knocked and Masaru hurried to receive them.

"Good evening, Munai, I'm Nissa Berdat, and this is my assistant Mae-uhkel Granahoi."

The dazzling heart of the Boehara revealed he was the Voluxian Khalil. "A pleasure, Munai Takashi, I'm a final year student of Applied Psicophysics and have followed your research closely."

"Yes, Mae-uhkel is here to translate for me," Nissa added laughing. "We come from TUUS World Network and, as I mentioned, we are interested in learning about your ideas and advances in energy matters." The Munai received them enthusiastically, and they started the interview.

"Wow, TUUS, we watch it a lot in Lukón... But please come in, sit down. My daughter Etzuko already told me something, how nice, take a seat, I just had a sudden but fleeting joy."

They began talking. While Munai explained what had happened and how suddenly his financial aid was cut off, Nissa and Mae-uhkel look at each other, seeing this as a confirmation of the conspiracy but they didn't interrupt. The Munai continued explaining then his theory of what was occurring, Mae-uhkel listened attentively, thinking ahead about the best way to approach Munai. What would he say? He took a deep breath and waited for Munai to pause in his speech, meanwhile wrapping Munai in a white and golden light, enabling him to elevate his internal understanding, and threw him an unexpected question. "Munai, I'm going to ask you a question that might sound unusual and off-topic, but it's really not, just try to follow me," he said. "Do you think there is a Superior Intelligent Power?" The Munai was surprised by the young huno's question, and Nissa didn't understand anything either, but Mae-uhkel continued unperturbed. "Look, I'm not referring to the Gaemo of religions, but more of a Supreme Order, a Great Intelligence or Master Mind. Nature itself, but as an intelligent force... and I ask because if there is a Supreme Intelligence that is perfection, then randomness would be an illusion... You say that it seems you are obtaining results that do not obey any pattern, right? But what if there really is a pattern or law behind it that we are not yet capable of understanding? What about the Law of Uncertainty and if something is happening at the quantum level that we simply, so far, cannot explain or parameterize? I've always thought that chaos does not exist, it's our inability to explain phenomena and include all variables in a coherent algorithm."

Takashi was thoughtful and then replied hesitantly: "Hmm, interesting concept..."

"Of course, Munai, perhaps the mistake is to continue separating the concepts of Science and Spirit when they are One. It may sound esoteric, but think about it. What if we used science to understand Gaemo, Gaemo which is nature itself, which is Science itself. Munai, for example, the Filament Theory... What do you think of it?"

"That it is very interesting and in fact is the one that best explains phenomena until now 'unexplainable.' It integrates the micro with the macro..."

"Exactly," Mae-uhkel interrupted, "it seems, according to that theory, that Everything has life..." "Wait, wait, how's that?" asked a skeptical Munai.

"What I mean is that, according to that theory, everything in the universe is, and in general, we are, nanocords, filaments vibrating at different frequencies, right? Therefore, we are all made of the same thing, then everything is connected. We are like a large energy network connected by invisible threads. The sensation of separation is a mirage of our limited senses, every action affects the Whole. So, everything we do, think, say, and even feel has a repercussion, an effect... "Well, it might be, but I still don't understand your point," replied the Munai, still confused. Mae-uhkel wasn't sure where he was going either but continued speaking from the wisdom he had recently rediscovered and as if inspired by an unstoppable internal force. "Look, Munai, maybe the piece missing from your puzzle has to do with that fact... Everything is alive and connected, there is no effect without cause, perhaps thinking about that will help you. I mean, thinking 'out of the box.' Remember that the known path doesn't always lead us to our palace; maybe letting go of the old and daring to try the alternative path will lead us directly to it."

Immediately Takashi remembered his dream where he was driving in circles for taking the – safe – 'path'. He also remembered that in it he was going to... – A palace! – It had to be a coincidence. Takashi's surprised face, combined with Nissa's disapproving expression, made him think he was losing Munai's attention. He cut his exposition short, thanked Masaru for his time, and ended the interview as well. Nissa, still not understanding but following her friend's instructions, didn't say a word and upon leaving asked: "What was all that about? That one was the worse 'interview' I saw in my whole life, the only that talked was you, you just made one nonsense question and then began speaking non stop..."

"I really don't know," Mae-uhkel honestly replied.

"What… you don't know? Wait," she said, stopping abruptly and turning her gaze sharply towards her friend, "but I thought you had everything coldly calculated, that it was part of a plan for your Thesis… 'Nissa, let me talk,' you told me, and now you're telling me you don't know?"

"Nissa, I really said what I felt I had to say, no more. I certainly think he didn't believe anything I said, but we'll see, we'll think of something." Nissa grabbed Mae-uhkel by both arms and, looking deep into Mae-uhkel's eyes with a fiery gaze that struck him like lightning, said:

"Mae-uhkel, honestly, until now I've done everything you asked of me and always trusted you, but I truly feel it's you who doesn't trust me. I moved the world and Dahna to get this interview, and you're improvising… I can't believe it. Why do I feel like you're hiding something from me? I need to know the truth right now if you want us to continue together in this."

Mae-uhkel found himself between a rock and a hard place. How could he tell Nissa the truth without her thinking he was crazy? Full of anxiety he took a breath, but the tension of the moment made him forget everything he'd learned, and intimidated by his friend's firm attitude, he spoke:

"Okay Nissa, but let's sit down because it's a long story and I don't know where to start. Do you remember when you called me a 'little wizard' because I knew Munai Takashi was in Akuahgrandia? Well, the truth is that since I was little, I can see and hear things that no one else can. Please don't think I'm crazy. I know Zaver will win the elections, I know Munai Takashi will finally make his discovery, and you must disclose it to the world to prevent the war between Z-suní and Deilgohu that would mean the start of a thermonuclear war and the extinction of the hunuman race," he blurted out all that, squeezing his eyes shut, waiting for a response.

*https://opensea.io/collection/another-world-the-book*

Nissa, who had been staring at him intently, was silent for a moment and then replied:

"Hmm... so the real reason you've had me working like crazy is... this superhero and villain's tale you just told me... are you serious? This is outrageous," she said standing up and visibly upset. "But I deserve it, why, why am I always so naive!!!??... And now, what about my reputation in front of the Munai? Oh, my Gaemo! Don't you think you're a bit too old for these things, Mae-uhkel? It can't be! IT CAN'T BE! ... you know what?!, I'm sorry, but no, I can't continue. This is it, you helped me, I helped you, and that's all. Please don't call me again about anything to do with Eco Synthesis, psychic powers, or the end of the world because I really have more real problems to deal with." She took her purse and left grumbling, leaving Mae-uhkel sitting on the bench at the Major School, feeling like he had failed in everything. Galek surrounded by darkness, unable to convince Takashi, and driving away Nissa; he didn't realize how, but he was worse off than at the beginning, alone and clueless about what to do.

However, what both didn't know was that Munai Takashi was deeply moved by Mae-uhkel's words and their coincidental relationship and similarity to his dream. That evening, at home, he meditated on the sofa about all of it; "the alternative path, leaving the old behind. Could that be what leaving the vehicle symbolized; leaving everything that had brought me to this point and trying a new approach. 'To proceed on foot.' Hmm…" Pondering this, he fell asleep. Once again in his recurring dream, this time when he reached the fork, he decided to get out of the vehicle, leave it there, and take the path on the left. This path led him into an intricate thicket full of exuberantly beautiful but strange plants. He felt a little anxious and fearful, as this route looked more winding than the road, but this changed immediately. After passing the strange bushes, his view opened to a beautiful jungle of lush trees with thick trunks, intimidatingly large, giants that seemed to have centuries of life. He noticed things he had never seen before: unknown plants and animals of many radiant colors. After a while walking in the middle of the peculiar forest and without realizing it, he found himself very close to the beautiful Palace he was heading to. Only a lake of crystal clear ákuah stood between them, so clear that the color of the bottom could be seen, and in combination with the blue sky formed a turquoise color that amazed him; he stood contemplating it for a while. Suddenly, the inert lake seemed to come to life, with many beautiful forms like vortices rising into the air. It was a fountain dancing to the rhythm of a celestial melody.

*https://opensea.io/collection/another-world-the-book*

A magical and beautiful spectacle, the ákuah seemed to have intelligence, to follow the music, to be alive; at that moment one of the vortices approached him as if inviting him to take a step and ride on it... he hesitated at first, but then let himself be carried away on the dancing ákuah, floating and sliding straight to the door of the beautiful Palace. There, the vortex carefully placed him in front of it. He tried to enter, but the door was closed, and an elaborate lock indicated that he needed a key to open it. As he looked around for the precious key but found nothing, he heard a voice in his head "Look in the ákuah, the secret lies in the ákuah." Turning his gaze back to the lake behind him, he saw a glow at the bottom near the shore. He approached the lake in that direction, walking along the small beach formed by the ákuah with the palace island. The glow came from a chest that shone submerged near the shore. He took it and opened it carefully. Inside was a key as exuberant as the lock; with it, he hurried to the door. He inserted the key excitedly and slowly turned it, opening it as he felt on his shoulder... the hand of his daughter, who was waking him up. "You fell asleep on the sofa, dad," Etzuko said. Masaru looked at her and said: "The secret is in the ákuah. Everything is alive..." and repeating this idea to himself, he went to bed. The next thía, upon arriving at his office in the laboratory, he sat down at the proccuan intending to delve as deeply as possible from all perspectives into understanding ákuah. Exploring the knowledge of the liquid on GlobaNet, he read things he already knew, such as the peculiarities of ákuah as a compound but, to tell the truth, he had not paid attention to it and reflected that yes, ákuah behaved very peculiarly and differently from the rest of the elements in nature... It was the only element that could be found in solid, liquid, and gaseous states. Denser when cooled, but from Four Termos downwards it becomes less dense. It has a high and unusual surface tension, is the universal diluent, a very high boiling point, but until now, to tell the truth, he had not paid attention to all this nor believed it was relevant. Then he found an article about ancient civilizations where it was claimed that, from antiquity, philosophers and hunos of science considered ákuah a gift from Gaemo, 'The Driving Force of All Nature.' He remembered Mae-uhkel and his words and his thoughts went in that direction, then with his attention on that Great Intelligent Force they talked about the thía before, he wondered what this wonderful element had to reveal to him. He got up from his chair and wandered around the laboratory in search of ideas. Walking back and forth inside the same laboratory, he threw hypotheses and ideas into the air which he then discarded; when passing by the small library of the laboratory, something caught his attention. Among the pile of old reports of work done at the same Major School, one of the volumes was titled *'Detection and Analysis of The Structure of ákuah'*. "The Structure of ákuah?" It was a concept he had never heard of. He took it; the dusty volume seemed to have been untouched for several cycles, the dedication read: *"To my wife, who inspired me to think Out of the Box."* He was excited to see the phrase, too many coincidences, then his interest grew, and he continued reading. What the old report revealed was both shocking and disconcerting. The experiment recorded a simple way to make visible the structure of ákuah: by applying drops of ákuah to slides and looking at them with a dark field microscope. But there was more; while the individual drops made by different students were different from each other, the drops made by the same student repeatedly showed a similar image in the dried ákuah drop. He thought for a moment it could be due to the composition, but after continuing to read, he realized that they all had the same composition. Then he went to the bibliography of the study and was surprised to discover that the same Munai who led the team that did the work had several publications related to the study of the structure of ákuah. He quickly noted all that seemed interesting to him and headed to the main library of the Major School. There, with notable enthusiasm, he gave the list to the surprised librarian who couldn't remember having such a passionate client in the four cycles she had been working there. He took the pile of books and sat down to read avidly. He found that the same Munai, but with another group of researchers, using Nuclear Magnetic Resonance, discovered that – the Akuahs – resonate at different frequencies and this was due to structural differences in the ákuah... Apparently, more than the chemical composition, the structural composition of the essential particles of ákuah and how they were organized among themselves made ákuah behave in particular ways. The more he read, the more interesting the topic became: "The essential particle of ákuah, composed of two Trisfacio nanomos and one of Ucceno, is what most of us consider ákuah. The real picture is a bit more complex. Its essential particles seem to be very gregarious. They like to gather and are rarely found alone. They will group into clusters of different sizes and shapes, from five to more than six hundred essential particles, giving ákuah different properties. These groups are not static. The essential particles of ákuah will change from one group to another very easily and will do so frequently. The trisfacio bonds are formed and broken several times in nanoquarts. This creates an unimaginably dynamic energy environment for ákuah. The size and shape of these clusters of essential particles in their incessant interaction is what is known as 'The Structure of ákuah.' "Could it be in this 'Structure of ákuah' where the missing piece lies?" His thoughts were interrupted by the sound of his nokó: "Hello!?" answered the Munai, on the other side there was no response, however, the breathing in the background denoted the presence of someone on the nokó who only listened. "Hello, yes, Takashi speaking!" he said again while the caller remained silent for a few more moments and then ended the call. Puzzled, Takashi checked the nokó, the nokó code was hidden. Nervously he noticed it was already dark, looked at his krono, dahna had fallen, he gathered the pile of books and prepared to leave. On his way to his vehicle, he noticed that the dahna was particularly dark, which made it difficult for him to find his keys and to maneuver among the books, his briefcase, and his jacket, all of which he carried in his hands with difficulty. Amidst this, he did not notice that he was being followed by a tall huno who caught up with him just as he reached his vehicle, suddenly grabbing him by the shoulder from behind.

https://opensea.io/collection/another-world-the-book

"Hey!" Masaru was startled and turned around abruptly. "Your keys..." It was the library's security guard who had followed him after noticing he had left his key ring on the table where he was reading moments before.

Masaru breathed a sigh of relief, thanked him, got into his vehicle, and drove away.

The next thía, in his laboratory, he continued his research, which became more fascinating the deeper he delved into it. One of the Munais claimed that these clusters of essential particles he had read about the previous thía acted like a type of memory cell in which the ákuah records the entire history of its interaction with the world, like a magnetic tape. *Ákuah had memory.* And the next fact was as shocking as it was disturbing:

Cycles ago, during the Great War, a group of researchers from Z-Suní was gathered in a room, heatedly discussing the development of bacteriological weapons. Suddenly, all participants began to show symptoms of severe food poisoning. They managed to call the paramedics, who tried to discover what had caused the poisoning. But the only thing the participants had consumed in common was the ákuah on the meeting table; the poison had to be there. However, when the ákuah was chemically analyzed, it was found to be pure and free of harmful contaminants. Its chemical composition was normal. The report then concluded: "Poisoning caused by common ákuah."

Masaru was astounded; the report could be suggesting that the ákuah had assumed the lethal properties of a weapon just by being exposed to the idea. If so, the implications of this were immense. But he was more surprised by how these findings could have been ignored by the Scientific Community, despite the involvement of renowned researchers and even those awarded top international prizes by the academy. He became pensive, and suddenly his absorption was startlingly interrupted by the ringing of his nokó:

"Takashi speaking?" An odd voice, electronically altered, responded:

"Munai, stop your research, value your career and your life, save yourself from ridicule... or something worse..." and they hung up.

"Hello, hello, who's speaking?" The call made Takashi realize for the first time that the cutting of his funding in Lukón and the inability to find anyone to support him afterward were probably not isolated or *coincidental* events. Perhaps someone wanted to prevent him from succeeding. He was afraid, was giving up the most appropriate option? But he was so close. At that moment, his gaze passed over the books he had open on his desk, and his eyes were drawn to a very particular phrase, 'dead ákuah'... he read the article hurriedly from the beginning to see what it was about. The phrase belonged to a statement made by an award-winning scientist that left him perplexed: "The well-known 'Memory of ákuah' is nothing like they want to make it seem, they are essential structures that mimic the information to which the ákuah has been exposed. It's not pseudoscience. It's not charlatanism. These are real phenomena that deserve more study..." surprised, he paused to absorb what he was reading. It was too important, then he continued: "...despite what you may have heard, much of the tap ákuah, deionized ákuah, and even bottled ákuah have very high acidity levels. The long-term effect of this acidic ákuah is that it causes the accumulation of free radicals in the body, which are the source of aging, generation, and growth of abnormal cells, and the destruction of healthy cells. Most filtration systems can not only remove almost everything from the ákuah, but they also remove its vitality, leaving us with, essentially, 'dead ákuah'. "DEAD ÁKUAH!" Now everything was beginning to make sense, Mae-uhkel's speech, his dream, the 'Living ákuah' ... Then, as if possessed by an uncontrollable impetus, he went to his proccuan and started looking for ways to – revive ákuah. –

After a short while, he found something.

Cycles after the Great War, Torvik Muchic devoted much time to developing a device for the production of 'living ákuah,' that is, ákuah with a reconstructed structure that also contained all the necessary minerals. According to his theory, spring ákuah is the optimal choice for life and health, as it emerges from an environment that preserves its natural balance state. But, due to hunuman action, the number of intact ákuah springs has been reduced. On the other hand, the structure of ákuah is destroyed by the effect of unnatural movement through straight pipes made of artificial materials. Muchic's device was based on a simple but very powerful theory, 'Ákuah is an information carrier and increases the quality of its structure by passing through a vortex or whirlpool system!'" "THE VORTEXS OF HIS DREAM!!!" Masaru trembled with emotion, feeling the adrenaline of excitement run through his veins as he realized how all the pieces were beginning to fit together. Like someone reading a suspense and adventure novel, he dived back into his study: "The Spiral is the quintessential natural pattern, galaxies, snails, seeds, the progression series of the Ohmas Number. The movement of nature for all construction processes is based on the prevalence of the traction principle. If the natural vortex movement is adequately copied, powerful suction forces that are capable of generating, very quickly, huge amounts of energy can be released with very little effort. But for this, a simple whirlpool is not enough, there must be multiple. These flow independently and at different speeds towards the center of the main vortex, each time at a higher speed, producing suctions towards the bottom. The essential particles of one speed level suddenly change to the next faster speed level. The cluster structures do not withstand the pressure differences, the complex essential structures decompose into smaller ones and begin to release enormous forces. Intense whirlpools can also dissolve the recorded information field in ákuah and produce Hexagonal Structures returning life and natural condition to ákuah..."

Reading this, Munai Takashi became thoughtful, wandering again through the laboratory. Everything was too interesting, but how could all the information he now had help him in his work? Absorbed, he served himself a Shazaá, then another and another, pondering. Would it be that if we use this 'Revitalized ákuah' as a medium in the electrolytic cell...? But as this idea came to his mind, the stimulating drink opened his mental field enough to let in an idea of fear and doubt projected by one of the Tumsas that always lurked around the five chosen ones, in a perennial attempt to prevent the completion of their respective missions. Assuming the idea as his own and as part of a possible fear of success, he thought: "Should I stop everything here? He felt a desire to tell Etzuko about the mysterious calls, but then desisted from the idea. He didn't want to worry her or worse, involve her and harm her. Better I stop... but I'm so close... the mere idea that structured ákuah worked was too strong. It resonated too much in his heart, and finally, after several thías of internal tribulations, his desire was strong enough for Takashi to ignore the threats and set out to find the plans of Muchic's device. He studied them in detail and managed to build, in a rudimentary manner, a replica of it. When it was ready, he annexed it to the tank of the cell so that the ákuah would pass through the revitalization system before entering the electrolysis process.

He set out to test it, but first, he closed his eyes and remembering Mae-uhkel, who, with his words, had ignited within him the flame of this new idea, said:

*https://opensea.io/collection/another-world-the-book*

"Supreme Force, I dedicate this to the good of hunumanity." And he turned on the prototype… In a few moments, a blue-golden flame shone as it had before, flickered, as it had before… but, wait… this time… it did not extinguish, it kept burning. Masaru held his breath, trying not to move so as not to influence, but the flame, although wavering, was stable and permanent. As time slowly passed and the combustion remained firm, finally, the Munai exhaled, it was the rest of success; tears began to well up in his eyes, and he fell to his knees with his gaze fixed on the living flame, a symbol of the conquest of a lifetime of work and research. The image of the young huno with his questions fixed in his head, he silently thanked him so many times at those moments. Eco Synthesis was a reality, a gift to that hunumanity that needed it so much without knowing it.

# CHAPTER VIII

## TOGETHER AGAIN, WELL, ALMOST...

The tension in Akuahgrand society was so intense, due to the uncertainty of the election, that it could almost be felt on the skin. It was such that it left the official authorities very few thías to find a way to alter the results, the popular pressure was unstoppable. There was a kind of awakening among the population that no one could have foreseen in a society, a few conjunctions before, politically apathetic. People began to demand results, through different means, in various places, and more and more joined the clamor that became widespread. They showed up at the polling stations and the electoral authority's headquarters, at the regional and national government houses, demanding audits, and the streets were filled with the Akuahgrandian people demanding their rights. A situation that, because of the suddenness of its development, took everyone by surprise, especially the governing elites. They thought that after a few thías, things would be forgotten as always, and they would continue as before, but it was not so; on the contrary, with each passing moment, more and more joined and remained, sleeping in the streets in a beautiful demonstration of the power of the people united for a common cause. Finally, the Electoral Tribunal was forced to declare the results as they were, preferring to do so and then resolve things as they went along rather than deal with a popular rebellion that was already beginning to seem imminent. The entire nation was watching the RB, and of course, Nissa too, from the newsroom of the channel. There, news arrived that Kelia would lose and that Ragner's lead was increasing. The result was a surprise to everyone, even more so for the young news reporter, to whom Mae-uhkel had already predicted the outcome. "The numbers..." they said "...were very close, and that's why it took us so long to give definitive results. However, with all votes counted and a very small difference between the first and second place, the new Magnhuno of Akuahgrandia is the galar... sorry, The new Maghhuna is the galera Kelia Zaver..." The biggest lie, the difference was overwhelming, almost seven to three, but they did not want to make the path so easy for Kelia; now that they knew they were defeated, they considered having lost a battle, but not the war, so they would do what they had become accustomed to doing in all countries that dared to propose a change in the global domination strategy. They would use all their wealth and power to infiltrate social movements, divide society, make the country ungovernable, and prevent Zaver, at all costs, from carrying out the changes she had planned according to her innovative ideas, not discounting the option, as they had done many times in other countries of the North of Hunum in the past also, of simply eliminating 'the problem' at its root, the political destiny and even the life of Kelia and all her allies was in danger. Nissa's nokó rang at that moment, still surprised. "Hello?"

"Yes, Major Berdat?"

"Yes, speaking, Munai Takashi, is that you? It's good that you call, I wanted to apologize for the other thía..."

"No Major, I called to talk with your young assistant."

"With Mae-uhkel? No, it's not necessary Munai, I've already talked to him about it and I assure you he's clear..."

"No, please, I insist, I need to thank him..."

"Wait a moment..." Nissa interrupted, frowning "thank him? But why?"

"Yes Major, thanks to that young huno we succeeded, his words led me to the key, we have Eco Synthesis..."

"Nissa was frozen, now indeed in shock. Mae-uhkel was right, he always was, and she treated him that way... but then the story is real? And the implications of the discovery and what should she do now? she had a thousand questions in her head while Munai continued:

"You will have the exclusive, but please do not disclose the news yet," he asked cautiously considering the threat he had received, "I have to adjust some parameters first, I beg you for discretion meanwhile, I will keep you informed of all my advances... Hello, hello?! Are you still there?"

"Yes, yes, I'm here Munai," Nissa hurried to respond "sorry, I'm just still in shock, well I'm not with him now, but I will give him the news and your message. We are very happy for your success Munai, thank you very much for the call and for granting us the honor of being the first to bring this important news to the world."

"No thanks to you, young people, thanks to you... and to Gaemo, please tell him that, yes... tell him that Thanks to The Great Gaemo!!!" Nissa felt an impulse to tell him something more: "Yes, I will tell him... uh, Munai, one more thing," she added "please take care of yourself, what you have is very important and delicate."

"Yes Major, but do not worry about me now... we succeeded and that's what's important." Then Munai attempted to call Etzuko but quickly desisted, knowing she better would know about it when it became public for her own protection. However, he communicated with the candidate, now the elected dignitary, Kelia Zaver, to whom he also felt indebted for the support she had given him and because, thanks to her, he had obtained the necessary resources... He dialed:

"Nomocat or rather Magnhuna, first of all I wanted to congratulate you, this is Munai Takashi, from the National Major School, do you remember me?"

"Ohh, of course Munai, how could I not! Nice to talk to you. Thank you very much for your call. Sorry for the background noise, you know, we are still celebrating... but how is your work going?"

"Yes, I also called you for that, to give you more good news besides your victory, but it requires your utmost discretion. You deserve to know it since, thanks to your support, I was able to continue with my research. I think it could become one of the main levers of your government, however, I would like to keep the secret while I adjust some things... We succeeded Magnhuna! – "Munai Takashi, sorry did I hear you correctly? are you telling me you achieved Eco Synthesis? by the Great Gaemo, what an incredible news, today is a thía of good omens!... Tell me, do you have control of all the factors?"

"That's precisely what I want to adjust, but I'm sure it will be in the next few thías. Magnhuna, I know you are the most suitable person to give the proper use to this discovery. That's why I also wanted to tell you to locate the informatist Nissa Berdat, from the TUUS channel. She is a person of my complete trust and the only one, along with her assistant, who are aware of everything. She will keep you informed and is whom I want to give the exclusive... Magnhuna, it seems like a dream, you in the government house and this discovery. It feels like the world is beginning to change."

"Thank you Munai, it's an honor for me to be one of the first people to have the news. I want you to know that I feel a great responsibility now, to give it the best use and know that more than a lever for our government, it's a great gift for hunumankind, Munai. Your discovery does not belong to us, it belongs to the world and will change the course of history."

"Yes galera, well Magnhuna, we will then be in touch and let's stay celebrating."

"Thank you Munai Takashi and I also congratulate you, you are an exceptional hunuman."

"Thank you Galera, until then." The call ended. What neither knew is that the dark arm of the government of Z-suní, whose members were the main shareholders of the large companies of Sápea, had begun a campaign of espionage against the scientist. The calls were monitored and recorded in their entirety by the Central Intelligence of Z-suní, which had infiltrated Akuahgrandia with the consent of the outgoing government.

As the dahna deepened and after the coverage of the results had ended and she left the channel, Nissa, in the basement of the parking lot, took out her nokó to call Mae-uhkel, who, as usual, did not answer. Nissa reached her vehicle but felt as if someone had followed her. She turned around but saw no one, thinking it was her imagination, she got in and tried to call again before driving off, unsuccessfully. As she ended the call, she was startled by a figure who suddenly appeared next to her vehicle, tapping on the window.

*https://opensea.io/collection/another-world-the-book*

She turned around, alarmed, but then realized it was Galek. "Wow, you scared me..." she said as she rolled down the window. Nissa was surprised to see him, unaware of the emotional state he was in, and asked: "Did you finally decide I deserve your attention?"

"Sorry, but with everything that's happened, my father's death, the appointment... I've been very busy... I was just passing by the channel to check on some things, saw you in the car talking on the nokó, and came over to say hi," he replied with a somewhat distraught expression.

"Galek, I don't understand anything, why did you suddenly decide to avoid me and cut me out of your life without any explanation?"

"I didn't cut you out of my life, I told you I've been busy... and who were you trying to call, by the way?"

"I wasn't talking, I was trying to call a friend with whom we're working on a project…"

"It wouldn't be the one you met several quints ago at the Shazaá Lombardo?" he asked reproachfully.

"Exactly! How do you know? I wanted to see if I could meet him now, although I think it's a bit late..." she said, looking at her noko and krono at the same time, "to talk about it."

"And what's so important that you have to see each other at this time of dahna and can't be talked on the nokó?"

"For Gaemo's sake, Galek, really? Look, even though it seems a bit bold and unfair that after almost a conjunction of avoiding me, you now come to demand explanations about my life, I value our relationship and will give them to you… it's a work matter that's delicate to discuss over the nokó, that's why we need to meet in person. Besides, shouldn't you trust me and how I handle my affairs?"

"You're the one who doesn't trust me, having a 'project' with some channel maintenance guy and not even telling me… 'work matter' and you hold hands to talk about it? "

"Wait, wait… is this what it is all about? Ha, ha, ha, I can't believe this… ahh, now I understand… your disappearance and now this inquisition! Well, no, there's nothing to say, Galek. You're making up a story in your head where you're casting me in a very demeaning role of dishonesty," Nissa looked at him for a moment and shook her head; "I've explained what it's about, but if you want to make this into a drama, go ahead. So you know, when I'm dating someone, you in this case, it's because I want to, and when I want to end things and be with someone else, you'll be the first to know. That's how things are, but you and your jealousy are your own problem. See you later. – She rolled up the window and drove away, not before rolling it down again to shout:

*https://opensea.io/collection/another-world-the-book*

"BY THE WAY, HIS NAME IS MAE-UHKEL, NOT 'SOME MAINTENANCE GUY'," leaving Galek in an even worse mood than when he arrived. The young billionaire had never met a huna like Nissa, so free of thought and action. In his social circle, women tended to be submissive, modest, and conservative, making it very hard for him to understand his partner's attitude.

Meanwhile, Mae-uhkel was in his usual state of deep concentration. During it, his mind envisioned a scene with the five missionaries, gathered and holding hands in a circle, all with their eyes closed in a deep act of communion when, suddenly, a flock of black birds flew in from afar, disrupting the act with their annoying fluttering above their heads. Dodging them as best they could and without breaking the circle, they managed to get away, but then the impertinent birds encircled Fahel,

turning into a dark fog that formed a vortex, sucking him powerfully backwards, breaking the hand connection with Ooremis and Gheldar who, despite their efforts, couldn't resist the force pulling him away, culminating in Ooremis's desperate cry...

*https://opensea.io/collection/another-world-the-book*

The crows returned, attempting to encircle and attack the others again, but there Mae-uhkel felt the impulse to open his eyes, seeing the missed calls from Nissa. He felt it symbolized that everyone was in danger, especially Galek. He immediately returned Nissa's call. She answered: "Hello 'little wizard'…"

"Hello Nissa, are you okay?" he asked, concerned and puzzled that Nissa was calling him after what had happened with Takashi, wondering if something was wrong.

"Yes, of course, why?"

"No reason," he replied, relieved.

"Do you have time to meet now?" Nissa asked.

"Sure, but are you sure you want to talk to me?"

"Yes, I'll pick you up and explain in person."

When Nissa arrived, Mae-uhkel got into her vehicle, and she started by saying:

"Well... it's clear you were right," she began, "strangely, after so many thías and against all odds, Zaver won the elections, and... Nobody knows yet, but Munai Takashi is, still unofficially of course, the creator of Eco Synthesis" ... so... I owe you an apology."

"What?... I didn't know it had all happened already... and how? Does this mean you believe me now?"

"Well, Munai asked me to thank you, he said everything you 'didn't know you were saying' literally led him to the missing piece," she paused, then with a confused air expressed: "It's just so hard to digest, Mae-uhkel, understand, all of this is new to me. How do you know things that nobody knows, and even things that haven't happened?"

"Don't worry Nissa, I understand how difficult it can be for you and for anyone, but look, let me show you something," Mae-uhkel paused, then added, "I just need your full and complete trust to do it, will you allow me to see? do you trust me?"

"Of course, now more than ever, what do I do?"

"Just relax and allow me, I'm going to try to see into your mind, think of something."

"Nissa tried to think of something random, looked around, and saw her keys, so she thought of them." Mae-uhkel took a deep breath, then took her hand and clearly saw the keys in Nissa's mental screen, but at the same time, he also saw the entire situation with Galek that was on Nissa's mind at that moment, their old thías at the National Major School, how they had reconnected, her entry into the channel, their relationship and subsequent distancing, and the recent argument. He then understood a bit of the vision he had just had. "Okay Nissa, I don't know what doors those keys open..." Nissa was shocked and smiled, but Mae-uhkel continued: "However, sorry, I couldn't help but see more... and you should know something... Galek is an important part of everything we're doing, don't exclude him." Nissa was surprised again by the young huno's abilities, who had no reason to know about what had happened with her partner, though she was beginning to get used to it. She was about to say something, embarrassed by the possibility that Mae-uhkel knew he had been mentioned in the argument, but he stopped her and enveloped her again in lights of Truth and Light, continuing: "I need you to listen, please. What's happening with him now is not by chance and is due to attempts to separate us and remove him from the equation. I understand you might feel embarrassed by what I could see, but believe me, it doesn't matter to me at all, I know it really has nothing to do with me, we need to work together to get him out of the emotional mental state he's in. Nissa, Magnhuna Zaver, Munai Takashi, Galek, you, and I are more connected than you can imagine. Everything that's happening is part of a Higher Plan. We have to manage to protect and spread Munai's discovery and bring it to Zaver to disclose and share with the world before private interests get their hands on it or worse, hide it forever. That's the real plan, Nissa, there's no ideology or personal interest of mine in all this. We really have to achieve this for the sake of the entire planet," Mae-uhkel took a deep breath again and, taking advantage of his friend's openness at that moment, focused on the power of his heart, took Nissa's hands again and said, "See for yourself." A movie played in her head, allowing her to see everything: her Kalwaissan self and the identities of her companions Fahel, Pawqar, and Khalil, the Plan at The Center of Illumination, the words of the Messiah, all in a flash. Nissa broke into inconsolable crying, her hunuman self finally awakening to who she really was and what she had to do. Mae-uhkel hugged her, moved, and after giving her space to vent her feelings, smiled and said: "So… are you ready, Ooremis?"

In the thías that followed, Nissa wanted to calm things down with Galek, and they had agreed to meet at dusk to clarify the situation. However, Masaru, who had been dedicated to fine-tuning his prototype, creating an updated and improved version, and logging part of his handwritten notes and a complete and detailed report of everything on his proccuan, received an idea projected by a Tumsa to call Nissa that very dahna to personally present the device and schedule the interview to unveil the discovery: "Hello, Munai Takashi, a pleasure to greet you"

"Hello, Major, I'm calling to arrange the interview, and I also ask you to come with your assistant… what was his name?"

"Mae-uhkel, Mae-uhkel Granahoi."

"Yes, please bring Mae-uhkel. When is the earliest you could meet? I would like to share the news with the world as soon as possible; I've adjusted the parameters, and it's ready to be seen." "Sure, Munai, this evening if you wish" she offered.

"Well, better at dusk, I still have a couple of things to do."

"Perfect, we'll be there at sunset."

"Yes, perfect, see you here."

"Agreed, Munai, see you soon." After hanging up, Nissa was forced to cancel her meeting with Galek without being able to explain much, which he did not like at all and reignited dark feelings in him.

At the end of the afternoon and moments before the meeting, a person in the basement of the channel was finishing a snack, and a Tumsa projected an idea into their mind: "Throw the wrapper NOW!" They did so without a second thought. Shortly after, one of the electricians was leaving the facility towards his service van, carrying some boxes with equipment in them. The same Tumsa projected: "Walk on that side, so you can take a glance at those two hunas chatting over there..." He did so, puffing up his chest trying to catch the attention of the hunas who were chatting peacefully, unaware of his presence. Then, stepping on the snack wrapper left on the floor, he half-slipped, dropping some items from his box. This caught the hunas' attention, who laughed. The huno bent down, trying to pick everything up, but embarrassed in front of them, he did so hurriedly without noticing he left some screws on the floor, and continued his way. Moments later, Nissa left the channel, about to pick up Mae-uhkel from his music class to head together to meet Takashi on time. However, as she left her spot, her tire ran over one of the screws left on the floor by the electrician, puncturing moments later on her way to pick up Mae-uhkel.

Meanwhile, Takashi was fine-tuning details to welcome his guests: "Thank you, Gaemo, for allowing me to achieve this, fine-tune it, and leave this gift to the world. As he uttered these simple words, an idea came to him, really a thought transmitted to his head by his Gaema Guide: "Secure the new prototype and back up all data in the safe in your office." Following the hunch, he uploaded all the information to an online storage service, sending a private access link to Nissa and Mae-uhkel, took the new prototype, backed up all the information on an external storage unit, and along with his main notebook, stored everything in the safe in his office, adjacent to the laboratory. He then went back to wait for his guests. After changing the tire, Nissa picked up Mae-uhkel. He got into the vehicle and as they set off, he said: "We're late... I can't wait to talk to Munai, how did he manage it?" Focusing his mind on Takashi, he felt a void in his stomach, knowing something was wrong with Masaru. He told Nissa his feelings, thinking their delay wasn't coincidental, and, nervously, asked her to hurry.

At the laboratory, there was a knock on the door. Masaru welcomed them. "You've arrived a bit early, but better," he said, opening the door. When he turned the handle, suddenly a tall, burly huno burst in, surprising him, quickly tied him up, and made him inhale a substance from a handkerchief that knocked him out immediately. The huno took the original prototype that was still on the table, unaware of the existence of the second, improved version kept by the boehara in the safe. He made sure to erase all the content from all the proccuans in the laboratory, the office, and Munai's personal ones. He placed a different device where the prototype he had taken was previously. He positioned the boehara near the table and fled, closing the door behind him. Shortly after, Nissa and Mae-uhkel arrived at the laboratory of the Major School. They got out of the vehicle and walked towards the building when a massive explosion erupted on the third floor, where Takashi's laboratory was located. They rushed up the stairs, but it was impossible to enter because of the flames. Both began to scream Munai's name, but it was futile. The dedicated boehara had perished in the explosion.

*https://opensea.io/collection/another-world-the-book*

# CHAPTER IX

## VISIBLE WAR, INVISIBLE WAR

The next thía, the major headlines in Akaugrandia read: *"FAILED EXPERIMENT CAUSES EXPLOSION AND DEATH OF A BOEHARA AT THE NATIONAL MAJOR SCHOOL OF AKUAHGRANDI. – MUNAI OF LUKONESE ORIGIN, MASARU TAKASHI, PHYSICOCHEMIST, DIES AFTER HIS EXPERIMENT EXPLODES IN HIS LABORATORY – INVESTIGATING NUCLEAR ENERGY, SENIOR BOEHARA DIES"*

Nomocat Zaver was shocked by the tragic news; how could this have happened? The Munai had assured her that he had control of all variables, what could have gone so wrong? Were all his achievements also lost? She then remembered Takashi had asked her to contact the informatist Nissa Berdat. Maybe she knew something. Meanwhile, Mae-uhkel in his room, reading on his proccuan, knew it wasn't an accident and that they had deliberately ended the scientist's life. He was devastated, he had failed, he couldn't prevent the assassination and the destruction of the experiment, what would he do now? Everything was lost!

Then he remembered he had to try to calm down. He breathed deeply and as he did, he felt relief and peace. Moments later, while in that state, he entered meditation, a multicolored mist covered him, and from it emerged Khalil, beautiful and radiant as he had seen in his dream:

*https://opensea.io/collection/another-world-the-book*

"Hello Mae-uhkel, don't be sad, everything is fine, EVERYTHING IS ALWAYS FINE" Mae- uhkel was glad and tried to embrace him, but his arms went through the fluid and subtle figure of his friend: "Sorry, old friend, I didn't make it in time to prevent it…"

"It wasn't in your hands to prevent it, Mae-uhkel. Many cycles and lives ago, on my home planet, I carelessly and naively used science and caused harm to my peers. That same carelessness and naivety caused me not to be cautious enough and protect my life this time, even knowing I could be in danger because of what I was dedicating myself to. But don't worry, with what happened, my soul finally learned and grew. Now I am more cautious and careful, wiser, and all the experience has brought me a step closer to the perfection of the One. Moreover, the truly transcendental thing is the fate of Hunum, and let's be happy because the main purpose of my incarnation was achieved."

"Yes, but we lost it, Khalil, we didn't make it in time, and before we could disclose it, everything was lost," Mae- uhkel lamented.

"It's not, old friend. The information is backed up in an online storage service, you and Nissa have the access link in your Network Mailboxes. Also, in my laboratory, in the safe, you'll find everything you need. The word is AKUAHVIVA and... one more thing, please don't forget, they have ears and eyes everywhere, be careful as I wasn't," he said as the vision slowly faded.

Mae-uhkel took his nokó to call Nissa but immediately remembered 'they have ears and eyes everywhere.' "The lines must be tapped," he thought. "If so, they know about our relationship with the Munai, then how can I talk to Nissa without raising suspicions?" He concentrated and put his attention on her, he could see her mental field and connecting mind to mind, he placed a thought on her mind's screen. "I have news, confirmed it wasn't an accident, but our lines are tapped, we must meet at Lombardo, I'm going to call you on the nokó and when I say, 'I'm leaving,'

it will be the cue to let you know I'm heading there, play along, I'll call you Nissy as soon as you answer to confirm that this thought is real and not a figment of your imagination." He waited a few moments and then dialed. Meanwhile, Nissa received the thought, but doubted whether it was real or if everything that was happening was making her imagine things, however, her nokó immediately rang. "Hello, Mae-uhkel"

"¡¡¡Nissy," he paused. "I'm so sad, it's horrible, the Munai is gone!"

"Nissa recognized the keyword and confirmed that indeed, Mae-uhkel had transmitted that thought to her."

"Yes, it's true..."

"And all his research is lost"

"It's true, what a pity and what a loss for hunumanity."

"Yes, yes... what bad luck, to have something fail like that just when he had deciphered the matter..."

"Very regrettable indeed," Nissa agreed.

"Well, I'm leaving," he paused briefly again, "to the store and will stay home for a long time, I don't want to go anywhere else, I'm too scared."

"Yes, I understand, I feel the same. But I had to come to work."

"We'll talk later, thanks for listening, be careful"

"Of course, see you soon, Mae-uhkel." Nissa was thoughtful, then her nokó rang again, it was an unknown number, so she answered cautiously: "Yes?"

"Major Nissa Berdat?"

"Who's speaking?" she asked cautiously.

"It's Nomocat Kelia Zaver"

"Magnhuna?"

"Yes, Major, good thía, I'm calling about Munai Takashi, he..."

"NO, Magnhuna!" she interrupted immediately to prevent being overheard, "I'm sorry, right now I'm leaving for an appointment and I'm running late, please, can you give me a number to contact you later?"

"This same one, I'm calling from my personal nokó"

"Very well, wait for my call please, and again, sorry for cutting you off like this, but I'm in the middle of something urgent," and ended the call. Nissa rushed out of her office and entered a newsroom, where the phones were for common use, all this to ensure she was not being overheard, so she took one and dialed. "Magnhuna? Nissa Berdat," she introduced herself.

"Hello Major, did you forget something?"

"No, sorry for hanging up on you like that, I just didn't want to talk from my nokó. We suspect that the lines are compromised."

"What do you mean, Major?" the Nomocat asked.

"Magnhuna, we have enough reasons to think that the Munai was assassinated to stop his research."

"What? how? by whom? Are you sure of what you are saying, Major? It's a very serious statement. Do you have evidence of what you say?"

"We are working on it..."

"And his work and the results? The Munai called me moments before the tragedy asking me to contact you, that you were a informatist from TUUS he trusted and that, along with his assistant, were the only ones who had all the information. I hope we haven't lost everything."

Nissa really had nothing, but she knew from Mae-uhkel's telepathic message that they had new information, however, until she spoke to him, she didn't know what it was about or what to say, so she replied in a way to gain some time and keep Kelia's support. "Well, we are gathering everything we have and putting it together to see where we are, both from the Munai's experiments and his death. But you must know that it is a personal and strictly confidential project, Magnhuna, nothing related to the station I work for. I will keep you informed.

" Very well, that sounds perfect."

"Goodbye and thank you for the call." She finished and immediately went to meet Mae-uhkel. Already at the Lombardo: "What happened, what's new? I thought I was going crazy… how did you do that?

"It's a mind-to-mind connection, look," Mae-uhkel tore off a piece of a napkin, asked the waiter for a pen, wrote something, rolled it up, and before handing it to Nissa, he continued, "keep this paper with you, but don't open it until you feel the same thing you felt this time. It has a keyword that I'll tell you the next time I send you a message so you can confirm that it's not your mind but me."

"Very well!"

"Now we must continue with the plan, but we must be very careful. Nissa, indeed, the Munai was murdered, and the danger is much greater than we thought."

"But I thought we were finished."

"So did I, however, today I received new information. Check your Online Mailbox. The Munai sent you a link, he had all the information backed up in a private storage service."

"Nissa did and found the Munai's message, they both got excited, but when she clicked on the link, it didn't work. They tried several times and nothing, it said that information did not exist. "They deleted it," said Nissa.

"What? How? Can they do that?"

"Very easy, Mae-uhkel, if they could eliminate the Munai, tapping our lines… who do you think owns the GlobaNet and information companies? it's evident they erased the Munai's account… damn it, we lost it forever!!!"

"No, no… there's more, but it's in Takashi's lab…"

"Wait!, what?, impossible! Are you sure? Nothing was left there, Mae-uhkel.

"As far as I understand, there's something in the Munai's office safe. Maybe it's a copy of the experiment information."

"Okay, I'll go with you, but how will we get in? That area must be cordoned off."

"Hmm, I don't know, let's go there and something will occur to us…"

As dusk fell, they headed to the site, and there, inside the vehicle, they both observed the scene. Several police officers surrounding the area. All possible entrances were guarded.

*https://opensea.io/collection/another-world-the-book*

"What do we do now?" asked Nissa. Mae-uhkel thought for a while "Wait, I'm going to try something," he said, then closed his eyes and took a deep breath. Then he managed to leave his body that was sitting in Nissa's vehicle as he had done at Leyhana's house, but this time voluntarily. He flew straight to the laboratory. He toured it, everything was really dust and ashes, nothing seemed to have survived the explosion. "Poor Munai!" he thought. He went straight to the office inside the same laboratory, looked around. In that fluid state, the walls posed no obstacle, so after a brief search, he could see the safe behind one of the library's cabinets. He looked inside and saw the prototype, the notebook, and a disk drive. "Brilliant boehara!" he exclaimed upon realizing what it was. Then he left and thought he needed to find a way to get in and out without being seen by the guards. He took careful note of the positions of each one. There were two at each door of the building. One at the laboratory door. There was no way to enter through the regular paths. He left and took a general look at the Applied Physico-Chemical building, where the laboratory was located, then realized that it adjoined two other buildings. He thought perhaps the joint buildings would communicate internally through a corridor; he searched and indeed they did, but all those entrances were also under guard. He was running out of options. He returned to the laboratory, looked around. Then he noticed that the explosion had blown the windows' glass. He left through one of them and entered one of the adjacent buildings, after a while, he left, back in the vehicle, he observed how Tumsas surrounded his vehicle and were repelled by Nissa's Gaema guides. They had to stay as calm as possible to facilitate their protection by the luminous beings. He returned to his body and told Nissa: "It's the prototype, a disk, and a notebook, probably all the information from his research."

"Great! But how do we get it?"

"I have a plan, but it's risky, we need a large bag, and we must do it now, we are under attack and something tells me we don't have much time." They parked the vehicle in front of the adjacent building that was unguarded as it was just another building of the Major School. Mae-uhkel said to Nissa: "Ok, before we go in I'm going to show you something for your protection. Close your eyes, take a deep breath, now imagine yourself surrounded by a 'force field' of blue color that originates from your heart. That will protect you against invisible threats. You must stay as calm as possible so that its action remains active."

"Is that why you said we are under attack?"

"Exactly." Mae-uhkel did it for himself and for all the guards, to protect them from any idea that would put them in trouble. They entered acting normally. They went up to the third floor, there in the area of the boeharal offices, Mae-uhkel walked down the hall counting the doors with a gesture of his hand. When he reached the one he was looking for, he turned the knob and it opened, they both entered, then Mae-uhkel opened the window, they both came out, first him to help his friend. With many nerves, they slid along the ledge of the buildings. "It sounds cliché, but don't look down, keep your eyes fixed on my neck." They advanced along the ledge with relative ease, crossed at the corner, and continued until they reached the ornamental column of the main entrance which was wider than all the others; there they had to hug it with arms and legs to reach one of the laboratory's windows. They had to be extra careful because the target windows were also just two floors above the heads of the guards guarding the main entrance. With difficulty and almost on the verge of falling, they managed to pass, entered, ran stealthily past the guard at the entrance of the laboratory, and an instant before reaching Takashi's office, Mae-uhkel felt a shiver and his vision opened. He saw what, for its brightness in the heart, small and poor, seemed to be Tumsas touring the office, but these looked somewhat different..., in appearance and size, they were more similar to Common Invisible Beings, disembodied, but it was also unlikely because their vibration felt much heavier. One of them looked inside the safe, and the moment Mae-uhkel and Nissa entered, he turned and fixed his gaze on them, immediately the others did the same... Mae-uhkel didn't know exactly what was happening. The – beings – were still there, static, just observing them.

*https://opensea.io/collection/another-world-the-book*

Mae-uhkel closed his eyes, breathed, and consciously expanded the Blue Light from his heart which made them disappear instantly. They hurried to the safe. It had a kind of keyboard on the door and a small luminous screen that read "Please enter your code." Mae-uhkel wrote 'ákuah viva' , but nothing.

"It can't be!" Mae-uhkel gasped.

"What's wrong?"

"It won't open"

"What do you mean it won't open?" asked Nissa with a knot in her stomach.

"The password was 'ákuah viva', I tried it and it doesn't work!!!..."

Something neither of them knew until that moment was that the Z-suní Central Intelligence had, since the time of The Great War, a secret squad, even for most members of the organization and the same Zetasunian government. They called it the 'Shadow Squad '. It was made up of agents with psychokinesis and remote viewing abilities, who were used for military and espionage purposes. Zaver's call to Nissa had raised suspicions, so they sent their agents to check the scene to make sure they had left no trace of the crime or the Munai's investigation. They were the ones Mae-uhkel saw prowling the office. Their protective action forced them out of their trance and back to their bodies, in the Intelligence Central office located in Z-Suní, thousands of kilometers away, they reported what had happened and from the central, they hurried to contact the authorities in Akuahgrandia. The time of the two missionaries was quickly running out. Meanwhile, they continued in their task, unaware they had been discovered: "Let me try," Nissa wrote all in uppercase "ÁKUAH VIVA", nothing... The screen blinked, "Last Attempt". Trying to not despair, Nissa took a breath and then asked, "is it a phrase or a word?"

"What do you mean?"

"That if it were two words or one..."

"Ehhh, oh, ooooh yes, right! the word... it's one word, no space," he smiled sheepishly. Nissa rolled her eyes upward in a gesture of frustration, then tried...YES! It opened. They took the box, opened it to make sure, the prototype still shined, they quickly closed it so the light wouldn't betray their presence with the guards outside, then they reached for the notebook and the disk, put everything in the backpack, and closed the safe. At that moment the guards were warned by radio and began to move in their search. The two felt the guards entering the laboratory. "THEY DISCOVERED US!!!" they whispered to each other simultaneously and hurried out of the office stealthily on their knees heading to the window. Hiding among the worktables and laboratory artifacts, they advanced toward their goal, evading the flashlights of the guards who were already inside the laboratory, heading toward the office where they were informed to look for the intruders. Little by little they gained ground and finally reached their escape route safely. Nissa quickly, but silently, went out the way she had come. She passed the wide column and when she reached the corner she crossed, but Mae-uhkel followed her more slowly, since he now had to be more careful as he carried the weight of the prototype and the rest of the Munai's belongings on his back. As he struggled to maneuver across the column, he lost his balance and stumbled. One of the guards felt the noise at the window and went ahead to look through it, but just at that moment Mae-uhkel crossed the wide column which served as a screen, fortunately managing not to be seen.

*https://opensea.io/collection/another-world-the-book*

The Central Intelligence was informed that the local guards found nothing. The Shadow Squad concentrated again. They appeared at the place, looked inside the safe. The Prototype was no longer there!!!, the chiefs in the concentration room asked the agents to move with their minds to the recently occurred moments and see what happened. Then they observed the whole scene, now they knew that Mae-uhkel and Nissa had taken everything, the prototype, the notebook, and all the Munai's research. As they drove away, Mae-uhkel checked the disk on his proccuan. "Damn, it's encrypted," he said.

"And can't you ask one of your 'invisible friends' what to do?"

"Yes, I guess, but I need to concentrate." Mae-uhkel closed his eyes, but at that right moment, they felt a bump in the back of the vehicle. They were being chased. "But how did they find us?" "Through the nokos," said Nissa. "Give me yours." Nissa took both devices and threw them out the window. From the vehicle chasing them, they then opened fire. "DO SOMETHING WITH YOUR 'POWERS'!!!" Nissa yelled, but Mae-uhkel was too agitated and nervous to achieve anything. "I can't, I have to relax"

"WELL, RELAX!!!" Mae-uhkel looked at her ironically and she returned a frustrated look. "Then I'll have to do something myself..." said the brave informatist and accelerated to the fullest. They continued in the chase, dodging normal traffic. Nissa riskily swerved into the next lane in a brilliant evasive maneuver, unexpected by their pursuers, a managed to lose them. They released the breath they realized they had been holding for a while and continued driving. When they both caught their breath, Nissa expressed annoyed: "Fantastic!!!, now we don't have fuel!!! "Let's fill up," said Mae-uhkel.

"I don't have cash"

"Me neither, but I have the card"

"Are you crazy?... so do I, but we can't use them, they would locate us immediately, we have to think" they stopped on a somewhat solitary street. They got out of the vehicle, went into what looked like a restaurante, and sat at the bar. There the site's RB was tuned to TUUS: "... The attack occurred a few moments ago, the Z-Suní Defense Department assures they had been following evidence for thías leading to the conclusion that the terrorist cell, with the support of the Deilgohu government, was preparing an attack of this nature, but had no indication of where or when. After this massacre, they have expressed their repudiation and say they reserve the right to take any action they deem necessary in the coming hours, to defend democracy and peace. – The government of Z-Suní, knowing what happened, considered it too risky to wait to recover the prototype and the information from the boehara's project and using a false flag attack, set the table to start the war in case the situation got out of control.

"It's a lie! They did it themselves!, Bastards!... they're setting the stage..."

"We're running out of time, Nissa, we have to publish this information."

"I know, but how? We don't have nokós, nor money..." Mae-uhkel got into the car and concentrated on his heart looking for answers on how to access the information to be able to publish it. He heard Leyhana's voice: "you don't have the knowledge for that, seek the support of the rest...". Mae-uhkel got out of the car: "We have to seek the support of the others..." Nissa looked at the fuel gauge, thought, and said: "I think I have an idea..." The fuel was enough to reach the TUUS plant. They entered and went to the floor of the live news studios. Nissa asked Mae-uhkel to open one of the maintenance doors and stay there, she said: "Wait here, stay hidden, I'm going to talk to Galek and ask him to help me get out a last-minute news"

"Be careful, try to inform the Magnhuna."

"I will." Nissa took the prototype and went towards the General Direction office, first stopping in the newsroom from where she had communicated with Magnhuna Zaver. She searched in the memory of the room's nokós for recent nokodes and there it was, she dialed: "Magnhuna Zaver? It's Nissa Berdat."

"Yes Nissa, tell me please"

"We don't have much time to explain, Magnhuna, I need you to listen to me carefully..."

"Then she left the office and went to find Galek. When she arrived at the reception of the floor, the assistant was going to stop her, but Galek saw her and signaled that everything was fine, to let her in. Nissa closed the door behind her, now she knew who it was and the forces behind Galek's attitude. She had to try to get him out of there for his good and for the mission.

"And what brings you here Major?" Galek said sarcastically.

"Love, please," Nissa immediately approached him, "let's drop this, shall we? I beg you, forgive me," she took his hands, "I swear that at first, I didn't understand anything, but now I see it clearly, you needed me to reinforce the fact that I love you and that I'm with you for everything you are, as a hunuman being, as a huno. Your kindness, your way of seeing the world, everyone as your equals despite life putting you in a privileged position. You are a wonderful being, Galek," she said as she hugged him, resting her face on his chest. Tears flowed from Galek's still lean face, and his armor seemed to start to crack at the loving words of his once beloved. Taking his face in her hands she continued, "Please, don't let them do this to us... we had something wonderful, don't let it be lost, I beg you..." they kissed and both remained for a while in a necessary silence, which said so much, but was broken by a question from Galek: "And what happened with the so-called project?"

"It's a long story and it turned out to be a super delicate matter." Nissa recounted what happened and Galek listened attentively while both remained holding hands, but, at the end, Galek suddenly let go of her hands and stood up. "And you say then that Mae-uhkel is here right now too? Did you come together?"

"Yes, he's downstairs in the studios.."

"And are you sure about everything you are saying, Nissa? It sounds ridiculous, like a 'conspiracy theory'." Nissa went to the table by the entrance of the young executive's office, took the container box, and pulled out the prototype in front of the astonished gaze of the young director "This is your conspiracy theory, do you believe me now?"

*https://opensea.io/collection/another-world-the-book*

Both left the office towards the studios. There Galek picked up the nokó and said to Nissa: "I'm going to ask for the live broadcast team to come. I'll go up to the booth to personally authorize the transmission. Look for Mae-uhkel and meet me here…" Nissa hurried to meet Mae-uhkel. They went together to one of the offices, where she related the plan with

Galek. "Mae-uhkel, I think I was able to touch his heart... I saw it in his eyes, but you have to do something when you see him, I think we can still rescue him," they continued walking and already in the office: "We'll leave the disk and the notebook here, we don't know the staff who will help us broadcast and although it's minimal, we can't trust anyone. You'll have the prototype off-camera. I'm going to go on air, to make sure we're safe and then after I've told the whole story, they'll have no reason to chase us, then you give it to me and we show it, turned on as proof that the story is true," Mae-uhkel was glad. "Come on, Galek is waiting for us in a moment in Studio Perie." As they left the office, Mae-uhkel said: "Wait," he went back into the office and came back out. "What happened?" "Nothing, I just went back to leave the bag and put things inside, we'll only take the box with the prototype, let's go." When they entered, Galek was standing in the middle of the studio. "Ok, Let's Go On Air," said Nissa, but at that moment two men took Nissa by the arms, two others took Mae-uhkel and took the box with the prototype from him. Galek pressed a remote control and a video was activated on the studio's monitors: "Citizens Mae-uhkel Granahoi and Nissa Berdat are both members of the terrorist cell The Way that claimed responsibility for the explosion at the Democratic Will party headquarters last Jurues. They are sought for their direct participation in the attack and are warned to be unstable and very dangerous people. Please inform authorities any information..." Galek turned off the monitors. "So this was the 'conspiracy' you both were fighting..."

"Galek, it's all lies, they're doing it to capture us and prevent us from revealing Boehara Takashi's experiment, you saw the prototype with your own eyes... please, Love, you have to believe me!!!"

"I believed you and I got you to work here, I believed you and became your 'boyfriend', but how could I be so naive?... you used me to get in here and give space to your comrades and that thing you have, surely it's a bomb like the one they put in Ragner's party headquarters... you're just an idealistic bitch, you always were..." Mae-uhkel, for his part, tried to use his energies to influence Galek, but with his vision awakened a few moments ago, he could see that he was completely surrounded by Tumsas and the Bham-yi of jealousy had grown almost to his height! In that state, nothing could penetrate him. The hunos took Nissa and Mae-uhkel away leaving Galek in the studio with a choked cry in his chest.

# CHAPTER X

## AN UNEXPECTED END

Outside, they were shoved into a van like vehicle, tied up and interrogated for a while. They gallantly endured the torture without revealing anything. After a long silence, a deep voice resonated from the darkness at the back of the cargo area where they were held.

"Granahoi, Granahoi..." he said as he emerged from the shadow where he had been hanging back and just observing. Approaching Mae-uhkel, the mysterious huno touched his forehead, but right away he knew his intentions and cleverly shielded himself with the Blue Light, preventing him from seeing anything. The agent furrowed his brow in confusion, not quite understanding why his attempt to read the young man's mind was failing, then he laughed ironically and said:

"Ha, ha, ha... good trick, you know? Truth be told, you deserve more respect than the previous one. It was easy to order him to do everything we asked. Very useful and obedient, that one... seemed to understand, for a long time, but at the end, his foolishness... his stupidity... came out... that you inherited. That's why we had to lock him up, to rot in that asylum. Ha, ha, ha... father and son, a pair of idiotic idealists, incapable of seeing such an obvious reality." The revelation that his father had secretly belonged to the Shadow Squad

and that his refusal to keep participating in its activities was the cause of his fatal end was shocking to Mae-uhkel--how little he knew his dad but how easily he had always judged him--but at the same time made him understand more about his torment. He felt compassion and shame. The agent continued, "They don't understand that NOT everyone deserves power, not everyone is ready for knowledge... 'people have the right to choose their destiny' the fool used to say when he refused that last mission... pure crap. People who live intoxicated, killing each other like wild beasts... those poor wretches, in their barbarity, don't know what's good for them. They live dominated by their senses, wallowing in their own filth, ignorant of how to direct themselves, what to do with everything they have." The agent, holding Mae-uhkel's head close to his face, asserted, "They need us, without us, they are just rats eating each other. Do you think, without our leadership, today we would be what we are? The pinnacle of civilization. Who do you think has always pulled the strings, rationing them, like children, the technology they can handle? We, their nannies, but now they want to be 'free', to have energy for all... to take control... ha, ha, ha... soon they would misuse it, waste it, and in a few cycles, they would have overpopulated the planet and consumed all its resources... Idiotic and shortsighted idealism... they need" - he emphasized "to be controlled, don't you see? For their own good and for all of us, hunumanity." Then he turned to Nissa, – "And you, huna," he said, "do you also have your tricks?" grabbing her head, Mae-uhkel shouted: "Do as I said!" She managed it and was able to shield herself, but it wasn't strong enough. Sustaining it against such a powerful foe proved too difficult for her. The agent sensed her weakness and persisted; she couldn't withstand it. The agent discovered her conversation with the Magnhuna Zaver: "…Send someone you trust to the channel immediately, tell them to watch TUUS and at the end of the broadcast where I'll appear, go to studio Perie, there I'll hand everything over, but if I'm not on air in the next few moments go straight to the office just in front of the main studio entrance and look on the desk. There will be the data and details of all the research. The safe's code is AKUAHVIVA, in one word…" The agent laughed victoriously as he exclaimed: "No, she's a normal one, stronger than expected, I must say… but normal after all! Hahaha. The code we're looking for is 'AKUAHVIVA'" They took the box, entered the code, and opened it. The prototype wasn't there!!! When Mae-uhkel met Nissa after his last encounter with Galek, he heard Leyhana's voice: "Leave the prototype here, let Nissa not know." That's what he really went back for at that moment. The agent let out a frustrated scream as he furiously hit them both, asking desperately, but could get nothing out of them, hurriedly called to report, and left them both unconscious with a blow to the head. As they regained consciousness, a worried and bewildered Nissa still wondered what had happened to the prototype. However, after a moment in which she seemed to stay attentive, her expression changed, and then, with difficulty, as she was kneeling and tied up, she took something out of her back pocket, it was the paper Mae-uhkel had given her, she opened it and threw it on the floor. Reading it, they both looked at each other and smiled complicitly, immediately one of the men grabbed her by the hair, dragging her to the center of the room where they were held. The agent pointed a gun at her and looking at Mae-uhkel said, "Another little trick, wizard! Hiding the prototype... ha, ha, do you really think you can keep it hidden for long, idiot?" However, the combative informatist, still struggling to speak due to the beatings, exclaimed: "Time..." she said, articulating her words with difficulty due to the bruises and blows, "... doesn't matter to you... because your time is already up! While you ramble on here, with your delusions of grandeur, our Magnhuna must be receiving in her hands, at this very moment, the prototype and all its data to reveal them to the world, Your empire and your hegemony are over!

He bit his lips in frustration for a few seconds but then his grimace turned into a mocking laugh and replied: " Ha, ha, ha, your naivety I think even moves me," he said mockingly, "listen, foolish... It's never too late when you have all the power! Only we decide when and what happens on this damn planet." Mae-uhkel could see through his mind that Z-suní had decided to fire its nuclear weapons against Deilgou and all its allies... they couldn't allow the free emergence of Eco Synthesis... "And if that's the case," he continued, "then you two are no longer of any use to us," and without thinking, he shot Nissa. "NOOOOO!!!" Mae-uhkel screamed just a second before feeling a shot in his chest.

*https://opensea.io/collection/another-world-the-book*

Different flashes of visions came to the mind of a dying Mae-uhkel, whose meaning he couldn't understand, with no apparent connection between them. Images of an arid urban landscape that seemed post-apocalyptic. He identified it as Hunum by certain buildings in ruins, and there, hunumans, including his perpetrators, seemed to have suffered long, chasing each other in a cannibalistic impulse, apparently caused by extreme and widespread famine. Then another scene... Galek walking as if in a hypnotic stupor, along with a group of others in the same state, all going up a ramp towards a large portal... and finally, a vision of Magnhuna Zaver standing at a podium, outdoors in an idyllic landscape, addressing a crowd of hunumans, all joyful: "It is an honor and a great responsibility for me to have been assigned this task of more than governing, serving the destinies of this new hunumanity, without divisions, neither social, geographic, nor religious. This new and unique country, the country of Hunum. Today we celebrate the return, finally, to our planet of origin, after all these cycles of preparation by the Fraternity of Light, and we want to pay tribute to the anonymous heroes who gave their lives to bring us closer to what today is a reality." This vision faded away.

*https://opensea.io/collection/another-world-the-book*

Finally, in front of him, the face of Ooremis with a sweet smile, who approached him gently caressing his face and with a look that transmitted much peace, let him know that everything was fine. He opened his eyes with difficulty, realizing that he was still alive and was being dragged, along with the lifeless body of Nissa, to be buried in a mass grave; they threw him in, first Nissa's corpse, then him, and as he felt the dirt thrown over his body, he thought once again that everything had been in vain, that they had failed, cried feeling disappointed, and asked for forgiveness... Then the image of the Wise Adelín: "... if their abominable nuclear weapons are used, which would

leave us no choice but to act directly..." Then Leyhana's: " ...just before the extinction caused

by those who led at the time, the great majority of the inhabitants, who didn't deserve to go through that horror, were taken off the planet and relocated to other worlds to continue their evolution." With Thía shining in his eyes and dirt still falling on his face, he managed to turn his gaze toward the sky, where immense and majestic ships—like those in his dreams but the size of cities—began to completely cover the hunuman sky.

*https://opensea.io/collection/another-world-the-book*

# EPILOGUE

## —THE END? —

After an indeterminate amount of time, Mae-uhkel awoke feeling different, lying down but so comfortable it was as if he was floating. Still a bit dazed, upon opening his eyes he found himself in a place so bright it dazzled his vision fresh from the darkness, and he could only make out a vague silhouette that caressed his forehead and said: "Welcome back, My Gheldar." Mae-uhkel wanted to ask what had happened, but he was interrupted. "Everything is fine, son, you did a great job, everything is always fine. Rest now, you're in transition, between your hunuman life and this one… there will be time to talk later." He closed his eyes again and fell into a deep sleep. When he awoke, still dizzy, he looked at his hands and his body while his still blurry vision adjusted to an apparently new condition, realizing that he was now in his Gheldar personality. Beside him, his guide, Ooremis, and Khalil. He was glad to see his companions again, but immediately noticed… "Where are Fahel and Pawqar?" Ooremis and Khalil exchanged a look of sorrow, and his guide intervened. "Both are still on a mission, incarnated as hunumans; I will show you." They helped him sit up, and his guide projected with a qelca the images. First, Galek appeared as he had seen while still agonizing as Mae-uhkel. "Yes, I saw this when I was still dying, but I didn't know what it was about."

"Galek fell victim to a condition in his character that still caused him disconnection, his pride and lack of self-love. These opened the door to the lurking attacks of the dark side, who turned him, without him realizing it, into an ally. His actions chained him to the third-dimension plane."

"Why is he in a hypnotic stupor, and where is he?"

"Z-Suní initiated thermonuclear attacks, and other powers responded. It was going to mean the extinction of the race and the destruction of the school planet Hunum, so we were forced to intervene. As it happened before, but this time globally. Galek and a small part of hunumanity saved from extinction are being taken to another third-dimension planet, according to their level of consciousness and with living conditions similar to those of Hunum before the attacks, to continue their evolution there. Fahel will remain in the third dimension until he understands and transcends the conditions that led him to act that way." Gheldar fell silent, showing sadness for the fate his friend would face and wondered for a moment if he had any responsibility in all this, to which his guide immediately responded. "Remember that everyone chooses their paths, my son, there's nothing you or anyone else could do. However, don't feel pain for him, remember that our Mother-Father is all Love and Mercy. His journey in the Light is indelible and will allow him to be one of the main guides of that population, which begins fresh on another planet and will surely have much to contribute to them, which will greatly help them to elevate and advance much in their evolutionary process. The Divinity will then be giving him another opportunity to return even stronger and closer to the One. You'll see that, in a few of our cycles equivalent to several incarnations in the third, we'll have him back, smiling and sharing with us his enriching experience." Gheldar understood and smiled, never ceasing to be amazed by the infinite beauty, compassion and mercy of the Light. His concern dissipated. "And Pawqar and the rest of the hunumans?" he asked then.

"As you can imagine, now the conditions on Hunum make life very difficult, as a consequence of the actions taken by its main destroyers. There only they remained, living the effects created by their own actions, as learning..."

"Cause and Effect," he thought.

"Pawqar and the rest of the hunumans who had developed the main virtues of the One: Love, Wisdom, and Will, to the adequate degree, were extracted and are being educated, trained by us outside of Hunum, in the most harmonious way of living, organizing, and taking care of their planet. They are witnessing from afar the consequences of all this time of neglect and the danger from which they were rescued. They will spend some time preparing with our help. These few cycles of learning and training in our dimension will mean several hundred cycles for their home planet, Hunum, which, sick from so much suffering, will remain in the third dimension during that time. This period will serve to purify the planet from so many cycles of mistreatment so that it can regenerate afterwards. Once this stage is completed, Pawqar in her personality as Kelia will be called to govern, along with a council of wises, the destinies of the planet Hunum, renewed, revitalized and already joined to the confederation of surpassed fourth-dimension worlds..."

Gheldar remembered the last of his visions, in which the wise diplomat spoke to a crowd and finally understood the complete meaning of his vision and smiled pleased and relieved to know the immense Love of the One behind the whole outcome.

...The System of Thías will finally ascend, and all its inhabitants will give each other a fraternal embrace, now consciously helping each other to grow and thus continue their path back to the Mother-Father. Thanks to you and all the thousands of other missionaries and conscious hunumans, the Light triumphed once again over the shadows, and thus the work of The Messiah Amina is consummated, bringing her children back to the One's path where Love, Wisdom, and Will reign in perfect balance.

This is the end of our story, but not the end of hunuman history, because for Hunum, it is a new beginning. And because this, just like all stories, including yours, does not have an end. It is eternal on the long path back to the light of Love. The most important thing is that it is not decided; it can change its course immediately as soon as you decide to see, to feel and to belong to *Another World*.

Made in the USA
Columbia, SC
05 November 2024